C000145230

The Sk Limit

A novel by Jamie O'Neill

The roses were in full bloom, and their delicate fragrance drifted across the garden. Elizabeth was sitting alone on a large beach towel in the shade of the apple trees. As she leafed through *Tatler* with only fleeting interest, the styrofoam cup of coffee next to her was becoming cold and would soon need to be replaced.

Glancing over the pages with blurry eyes her mind wandered. As early in the day as it was to be awake, these were moments she enjoyed. It was a Wednesday, it happened to be a day off, and it was the beginning of what would turn out to be a long, hot summer. At times like these it was enjoyable to simply lounge on the grass, breathe the fresh morning air, and not be forced to think about lists of tasks. Most of all it was a welcome break from worrying about the looming annual recurrent training that she expected would involve days of multiple choice exams, intensive late night cram sessions and practical assessments. All of it would have to be done on minimal sleep. She was astonished at how quickly twelve months of flying had passed.

Elizabeth yawned. She closed the magazine and checked her phone for messages. Her housemate Angela came into the garden from the kitchen with a fresh coat of sun cream on, her hair roughly arranged on top of her head.

'We should get one of those big paddling pools, you know,' she said. 'It'd be nice to come out here when it's hot like today, take a dip and cool off.'

Elizabeth looked up at the sky and noticed that there was barely a cloud.

'It's going to be scorching again,' she agreed. 'Where do we get a pool?'

'I might get one downroute, it'd probably be cheaper. I'm not sure if it would go on as hand luggage, though.'

Elizabeth smiled and turned to her drink.

'Do you want some tea or coffee?' she asked.

'I just had one, honey, and you're not at work,' Angela replied, after a pause adding, 'Well... if you're making one then I *will* have another tea, thanks a lot.'

Elizabeth walked into the kitchen and filled the kettle. She looked at the roster stuck to the fridge and checked through it to see if she had remembered her next trip correctly: Agadir, three day stopover. That meant packing for the gym as well as all the usual stuff. Since it was already summer, she was determined to keep in shape. It was not something she would ever openly admit to, but she knew that at peak fitness she was not merely beautiful, but stunning.

She was aware of the unspoken attention she received from many men as well as wary wives and girlfriends when out in public. When she travelled to and from the airport, the widely-maligned uniform actually enhanced the effect, and of course, being single, she knew that looking her best, which for her meant a little thinner than usual, would show her off in the best light.

Her dark blond hair danced around her shoulders as she prepared the drinks and she started to wonder exactly how Agadir would be. She picked up the wine glass that was standing alone in the sink, its rim marked with red lipstick, and placed it to one side. The standard of hotels the airline used was always very high, and according to other crew members she had overheard, the Royal Maluf was one of the best. Agadir was an established favourite destination in the airline, its beautiful beaches accounted for its popularity with the pilots and crew.

Carrying the cups into the garden, she noticed that Angela had stretched herself out fully across one side of the beach towel. She was smoking a long, thin Vogue, and now a little ash marked her bikini. She always admired Angela's lack of self-consciousness.

'Are you done with this magazine?' she asked.

'Go ahead, I wasn't really reading it anyway,' Elizabeth replied.

'Do you have plans for later? I was going to go to town for some new make up - want to come?'

'Sure. Actually it's been ages since we went. I need to get some stuff from Superdrug too.'

'Make up?' Angela asked.

'Mosquito spray and some Nytol,' she replied.

'Cool, you're on.'

Later that day as they left the Treaty Centre, Angela turned to Elizabeth.

'Shall we pop in there for a quick coffee?' she suggested, pointing at the café in the department store across the street.

'Definitely, my feet are killing me,' Elizabeth replied.

They took a seat close to the window, and the waiter, a young man in a dark green shirt, came over to take their order. Angela was debating with herself whether or not to order a slice of the Oreo cheesecake displayed in one of the chillers, however for Elizabeth cake was entirely out of the question.

'I'd like a black americano, please, and some water,' she said.

'An americano, a water...' the waiter repeated making quick notes in his little pad.

'Could I just have a latte, please?' Angela asked, resisting the temptation of cake.

'And one latte, of course. Okay, that shouldn't be too long, ladies,' he said, and walked back to the kitchen.

As he headed off, Angela took out one of her purchases.

'*Why Men Love Bitches*?' Elizabeth asked, overdoing the skepticism. 'I didn't see you pick that up.'

'My sister said it works, she recommended it,' Angela explained, flicking through the book. 'The checkout girl in Smith's gave me a weird look, but if it works... You have to try things!'

Outside on the high street, despite it being midweek, packs of shoppers thronged the pavement, brought out by the sun. In particular, lots of families with children seemed to be milling around.

'School holidays,' Angela said.

'No, I don't think so, at least not yet.' Elizabeth's eleven year old brother James was still at school, she was certain. 'So what kind of tips does it give?' she asked.

'Well I think the gist is that women have to be assertive. You can't act like a doormat and expect to end up with the right kind of guy.'

'So in theory, you want a gentleman?' Elizabeth asked.

'Who doesn't? Well, I mean gentlemanly in some areas, but dominant in others,' she started to whisper.

The coffees arrived.

'What do you think of Paul, the new guy?' Elizabeth asked. She was referring to the newest of the housemates, a Polish aircraft mechanic who had moved in a week earlier.

'I haven't seen much of him, but *too young* to be honest,' she said in a high pitch. 'I mean, I'm just going on first impressions here, but he's not my type,' she added. 'I do feel sorry for him living in a house full of women, though, and Sandra's not even back from Berlin. He hasn't had the pleasure of meeting *her* yet!'

'You want an older man, then?'

'No, just a guy who is manly, strong... but still in touch with his emotions. No cavemen. And no younger than twenty-five. A decent career, or at least ambitious.'

Elizabeth interrupted. 'Quite a list. What happened with Jonathan?'

Angela put down her latte.

'We went on a few dates, but come on. There's no way I'd get serious about some guy I met for the first time in a club. None of them are ready to grow up, I mean they can't be if they're still out partying, right?'

'Maybe they're not, but are *you*?' Elizabeth asked.

'Good question. When the right one comes along, I'll just know,' Angela replied looking thoughtful.

'You know what we should do?' Elizabeth said. 'I've always wanted to, but only if you're game, because I don't really want to go alone.'

'What's that?'

'Well, have you noticed that next to the big ASDA's there's that alleyway with a few run-down nail places and a few old grocery shops?' she asked.

'Sure, go on.'

'Near the end, there's a place with a sign outside for psychic readings. Mr Devi.'

Angela raised one eyebrow. 'Oh please tell me you don't believe in that stuff. You don't, do you?'

'I don't believe in it, not really, but I've always been

interested. And I've heard of people getting it right.'

'I don't have the money to waste on fake fortune-tellers.'

'I find that hard to believe when you've just spent over £150 on Mac.'

'Priorities,' Angela smirked.

'Come on, I think it'll be fun. Whether we get any useful information or not, at least it's something to do. Think of it as entertainment. At least we can say we went.'

'Okay, and supposing the psychic turns out to be the real deal, but he tells you something you don't want to hear? What if something horrible is going to happen?'

Her voice lowered.

'What then?' she asked.

'Yeah, I did think about that. There's only one way to know, and... whatever happens, you can't change it. It's fate, right?'

'I really don't believe in any of that stuff, but some things are just best not to mess around with. I know it sounds stupid. But okay, if you want to go, we can go for *your* reading. I might change my mind, but I'm not paying more than twenty quid.'

Elizabeth sighed. They left money for the drinks, picked up their shopping and left the café.

'You just said you have to try things, didn't you?' Elizabeth asked.

'Let's go to Mr Devi, babe, but any more than twenty means it's a rip off.'

'Please, my dears, come in, come in,' the elderly man beckoned in a weary, unconvincing tone.

They had paid at what served as the reception - £15 each in cash to the bored looking receptionist who looked as though he could barely be bothered to stand up. Aside from psychic readings, the small shop had all kinds of candles, incense, oils and books on sale. Despite having six chairs laid out, the main room was empty, dark and oddly silent compared to the street outside. It looked as though it had not been cleaned in years. Mr. Devi emerged from behind a purple curtain that was covered in dust, behind which there was a wooden table and some chairs that had been coated in fabric that could have once been white before yellowing over the years. He looked directly and intensely into Elizabeth's eyes.

'You came because you face uncertainty. Insecurity. This uncertainty leads you to question your path in life,' he explained in a deep Indian accent. Before she could confirm or deny anything he continued.

'My dear, all paths are open.'

There was a long pause.

'Show me your palms!' he ordered.

She held out her upturned hands.

'I do see a struggle which is unfortunate. You will face obstacles, but ultimately you shall triumph. It is written into your body, your fate. It is apparent that whoever tries to cross you will find their attempts to certainly be in vain.'

He leaned in closely.

'A person with vision - a man with a clear vision - will aid you in your journey.'

He then turned to Angela.

'My friend, show me your palms.'

His eyes widened.

'Ah, yes, I can see a past... A young girl sits crying alone at a window. Nothing but a pet to comfort her.'

Angela could not hide her disdain. Elizabeth imagined Angela was thinking that the word 'pet' was conveniently non-specific and the whole thing was a sham.

'She becomes skeptical, but in time truths are revealed,' Mr. Devi continued.

He looked directly at her, now with a very serious expression on his wrinkled face.

'Truth is revealed and the girl learns to *adapt*. This is all.'

For the first time he smiled at both of them as if to reassure them, and opened the curtain for them as they left, and almost inaudibly, he added, 'the sky is the limit'.

'Would you like to book a second consultation?' the assistant asked Elizabeth as Angela strode outside clutching her shopping bags.

3

It was early evening and a full flight lay ahead. At the briefing, the crew had rushed through speedy introductions, and the pilots, Tim and Justin, popped in very quickly to do the same. After a few easy questions about emergency procedures and first aid, Jane, the supervisor, began to frown as she looked over her printout.

'Alright then guys, we're going to be busy! Actually we're overbooked, so when we get on board let's get the security checks out of the way as quickly as possible and get everything ready in advance, okay?'

As far as pursers went, Jane was very pleasant. Elizabeth reflected on how she could often tell from the get-go which ones would turn out to be battleaxes or control freaks: there were a fair few in the company. She had the aura of experience, but also a friendliness, an approachability. In a way she reminded Elizabeth of her own mother, just in a more glamorous, made-up form.

'If there are any problems with the catering, just call me and Matt at the front, and we'll get it sorted out in a jiffy,' Jane said, nodding at Elizabeth, Fiona and David.

The three other, more senior crew members looked a little bored. Now and then they checked their phones, but Elizabeth was just one year in, and Agadir was a new place, technically her first stay in Africa. A little excitement had bubbled inside her despite the nonchalant and quietly confident appearance she was trying to give off during the briefing. Matt had to take a phone call outside and excused himself.

'Do you want to come to the shops in the terminal with me and David, Elizabeth?' Fiona asked.

'If that's alright with Jane, sure,' she said.

Jane glanced at her watch, nodded and smiled, and the crew left the briefing area.

'Let's all be at the gate for half past,' she said.

On board the plane, after passing through staff security and browsing the shopping area, Fiona, David and Elizabeth sat down together in the rear galley with a mini can of Diet Coke each.

'Go on, how old are you, then?' Fiona asked.

'Guess!' said Elizabeth.

'Oh no, don't do that to me... Well, alright. Twenty-one?'

'Eighteen,' David suggested and laughed.

'I'm twenty-three, nearly twenty-four,' Elizabeth said. 'I wish I could say I stay out of the sun and drink lots of water...'

'At least you're not pushing forty,' Fiona said with a wink.

'How long have you been flying?' David asked.

'It's coming up to a year now. Hopefully I've got the hang of it all,' she added with a shrug.

'When's your recurrent? I've got mine coming up next month,' Fiona said in an exaggerated tone of doom.

'Next month, too. Not looking forward to that. Apparently they make you redo the wet drills? I hate public swimming pools.'

David made a show of shuddering and Fiona stood up from her jump seat.

'Same here, but at least it's just one day,' she said. 'The exams are pretty tough, though. They let you fail once and resit, but if you have to resit a second time, it's quite serious. My memory's like a sieve, so I'm not going to get much sleep,' she added through the open toilet door, reapplying her deep red lip gloss in the mirror and then checking her teeth.

'The passengers are on their way,' Jane said over the loudspeaker, and a few seconds later the boarding began. Elizabeth took a position midway down the cabin to welcome the economy passengers and help them shuffle around hand luggage to get it to fit into the overhead lockers.

'She's nice,' David said to Fiona.

'Yeah, they usually are when they start off. Then as the years go by, you end up bitter and twisted,' she said with a smug look at David who was unfolding a paper booklet, preparing to read the boarding announcement.

'Speak for yourself, bitch!'

He picked up the interphone and held down the PA button.

'Ladies and gentlemen, a very warm welcome on board this flight to Agadir. Before making yourselves comfortable, please ensure that all hand luggage is safely stowed in the overhead lockers or underneath the seat in front of you.'

As he was doing this, Fiona started to prepare a bar top with ice cubes, mineral water and cartons of juice as an elderly man crept slowly to the rear galley holding the seat headrests along the way for support.

'Excuse me, madame, where is the toilet?' he asked as he reached the last row of seats.

Fiona stopped her set up and pushed open the door next to him.

'Thank you, thank you, my dear!' the man gushed.

'Can't people read?' she muttered to herself.

Matt called David from business class.

'How are you guys doing with hand baggage?'

'There's still a lot of room down here,' he replied. 'If you need me to bring anything down, I'll be up when the aisle clears a bit, just give us a ring. Cool.' He hung up the interphone.

'You know what?' he asked, feigning a confused look. 'I can't figure him out. Do you think he likes girls or boys?'

Elizabeth shrugged slowly. She had not consciously thought about Matt until now. As was usual, being junior she was never offered the choice of positions, and more senior crew preferred to work in first and business class with very few exceptions. This meant that most of the time she was left in economy. On busy flights, it was rare for her to spend much time at all in a forward galley which was where Matt was positioned.

But now she considered him. He had been polite, and although not at all macho, she did not pick up on the affected air that was common among other stewards. He had seemed a little distracted during the briefing. Or was he just bored?

'Did he mention a girlfriend?' she asked David.

'Well, we didn't have time to discuss that, but I'll be sure to ask him later!'

'Do you like them tall, dark and handsome, then?' Fiona asked him.

'I'm too old to be that fussy,' he replied, rolling his eyes.

'He is very tall, isn't he?' Elizabeth said. 'Isn't there a height limit? He must have just about scraped through,' she said almost to herself.

'At least six foot two. I didn't see a ring on his hand, but he's probably too young for that anyway,' Fiona said. As she was speaking, the elderly man staggered back out of the toilet and stood still for a moment as if he was collecting himself.

'Please, madame, some water,' he asked in a dramatically croaky voice.

Fiona passed him a plastic cup with some mineral water, a few cubes of ice and a slice of lemon from the row of cups she had prepared in advance.

'Thank you so much,' he said. 'Please, what is the captain's name?'

After a pause, Fiona replied, 'Tim Miller'.

'Ha, British captain!' the man said, ecstatic, before returning to his seat past the intimidating scrum of passengers building up in the aisle.

'And the stream of nutters begins. Girls, let's have a cup of tea, I'm already so exhausted,' David said snatching a giant teabag from an atlas box and flicking on the brewers.

'So how about you, then, David? I take it you're single, happy to mingle?' Fiona asked.

'Absolutely,' he replied. 'You?' he asked, turning to Elizabeth.

'Well, I split up with my ex just under a year ago, just as I started flying, actually,' she said with doubt.

It did not seem to Elizabeth as though it had really been a whole year of her life since then.

'Was that the reason you broke up?' Fiona asked.

'There were a few reasons, but I mean flying didn't come into it. At the end of the day, when it's not working, you have to stop and move on,' she said. 'We're still friends, kind of, but it just didn't work out. We didn't work as a couple.'

She was referring to Peter, her boyfriend through her last year of university. Peter, who, like her, was from a wealthy family, who had soft red hair and a delicate, aristocratic voice. She had imagined at one point that he was the one - the one she would start a family and grow old with. After a few months together, she could no longer deny the feeling that things were just not going in the right direction. Peter had grown too accustomed to her, as she had to him.

The predictability of his habits, their quickly-established routines, the overwhelming feeling of stagnation finally got to her, and the pair had mutually agreed to take a break in a bid to save the relationship after hours of painful discussions that would never lead anywhere. The break had ended up being permanent, and to her surprise he had moved on after a few weeks.

Elizabeth frowned and felt a little choke welling up in her throat. She did not want to dwell on Peter, but to deny there was no remnant of feeling would have been untrue, so she walked a little way up the aisle, forcing herself to smile and help people manoeuvre their carry-on cases, shopping bags and laptops in the overhead lockers which were filling up quickly, making as much space as possible in a concerted effort to take her mind off the past. It was working.

'Thank you, cabin crew, boarding is complete,' Jane said over the PA system.

All but a few of the passengers were now seated, and Elizabeth began to close the overhead lockers from the back of the cabin, Matt from the front. They met in the middle.

'Thank you, Elizabeth,' he said, reading her name on her badge and smiling down at her.

'Thank *you*,' she replied, and returned the smile before heading back.

In the rear galley, Fiona had started up the ovens. The passengers would want to eat a hot meal as soon as possible after take-off.

'What's on the economy menu tonight?' Elizabeth asked.

'There's lamb tagine or vegetable linguine. The tagine actually looks quite good,' she replied.

'Any specials?' Elizabeth asked.

'Just twelve halals, one vegan. We can run those out by hand,' she said.

'Just thirteen, not bad,' Elizabeth said.

'Here's madame's tea,' said David, handing her a paper cup and an airsickness bag that was full of sugar and sweetener sachets. 'It's very hot,' he added.

As the aircraft taxied towards the runway, the crew performed the safety demonstration. Elizabeth, in spite of herself, started to think back to Peter again. A few times she had mistaken a stranger for him at a distance and gone through her memories of the good times, the brief beginning stages of the relationship when everything had been fresh and exciting. It was often that you met the wrong person at the right time, or the right person at the wrong time. As she gestured to the exits she realised that a lot of the motivation in going to see the psychic had been to work out how to go on after such a total end: the end of her and Peter, and to a lesser extent the end of being new at the airline.

She enacted the correct way to use a drop-down oxygen mask. Those comments had seemed insightful, even if the man had made no concrete predictions. He had sounded optimistic, so at least she should be happy about that. A little girl smiled at her, utterly transfixed by the performance of the safety demo. Were the seeds being sown in her imagination that would lead her to go on to become a flight attendant one day, just because she happened to be awake at the start of this flight? And how did the reality live up to the dream?

A year ago, Elizabeth had been a wannabe, by her own admission. After sending off her application it had become a possible real career for her. And now, here she was, jetting around the world, spending time exploring places her office-based friends envied. There was glamour, that side of things was true, but at times there was also a lot of hard work and patience being tested. There was also the feeling of not being too new anymore yet not established, although new destinations still held a great appeal. And soon the recurrent: it felt too soon to be tested, but Elizabeth knew that in reality it wasn't.

When the demonstration finished, Elizabeth started her seatbelt checks, working her way towards the back row-by-row with David as Fiona secured the galley and toilets and emptied the tea and coffee brewers into the toilet. The plane began to taxi to its take-off position.

'I'm sorry, sir, you'll have to turn that off now,' Elizabeth said.

'My phone?' the man asked.

'Yes, I'm afraid you have to as we're taking off very shortly.'

'Okay, okay, just a minute,' he snapped back. She flashed him a broad, fake smile and continued the sweep.

4

The lift stopped, opened at the fifth floor and Elizabeth made her way to her room. The corridor walls of the opulent hotel were covered with purple and gold wallpaper, and in the air hung the subtle but unmistakable scent of the ocean. The room featured a giant, soft bed and overlooked a long beach, with a large balcony from which Elizabeth could watch the waves lapping gently at the sand while relaxing in one of the wicker chairs. A little way down the moonlit beach, she could see a bright red Moroccan flag flapping proudly in the breeze. It was a spectacular scene.

She set the alarm on her phone for eight to give herself time to do an early workout before a day of exploring. There was a text message from her dad: 'We're doing a big clear out, darling, tell us if there's anything you want saved. Love you and all that.' There was also a message welcoming her to Spain - she must have forgotten to switch off her own mobile before take off. Sure enough, the battery was almost drained.

Elizabeth started to run hot water into the trendy, triangular bathtub in the en suite and unpacked her case on the bed, wheels over the edge, as she made a mental list of things in her old room and the study back home that she did not want to lose. Having a surgeon as a mother meant she had had to learn to protect her possessions from frequent bursts of spring cleaning. Aside from a keen attention to cleanliness and tidiness, her mother frequently needed to make room for decorators installing constantly changing décor and new paintings and new sculptures, and after moving out officially the risk had gone up.

The phone next to the bed rang.

'Hello?' she said softly.

'Hi, darling, it's Jane, how do you like the hotel?'

'It's wonderful. My room's huge. Very modern,' she replied.

'Fantastic, isn't it? I think we're all meeting up in a few hours for a couple of drinks in the bar downstairs,' she said.

'Great, I'll join you down there, I'm just going to have a bath and chill out a bit. I'm off the alcohol, though. I want to get to the gym first thing in the morning. Did you get a seafront view, too?' she asked.

'Yes, it's gorgeous, isn't it?'

'I already don't want to go home!' Elizabeth said with a giggle.

'Right, I'll see you downstairs a bit later, sweetie. Dress to impress!'

'See you soon,' Elizabeth said, replacing the receiver.

She strolled over and poured an extravagant swoop of green Chanel bath foam into the huge tub and swirled the water with her fingertips. Her back had started to ache slightly, and her feet felt pinched from the uniform heels. Twenty minutes later, she had reached a perfect state of bliss and relaxation, basking in the steamy, luxurious aroma.

From her bath she was half-following CNN on the TV through the glass partition with the bedroom. A report on the downturn in the aviation industry came on which drew her attention, with footage of cabin crew training in New York. But rather than dwelling on the impending recurrent training, the report started to make her recall her recruitment process instead.

During the initial open day, the candidates had been asked to do a number of teamwork tasks for the recruiters to get an idea of how they worked with others. Elizabeth was proud of the fact that of her assessment day's selection of roughly one hundred hopefuls, she had been the only one to pass the one-on-one interview after that large, original group had been whittled down to just twenty.

At the end of the nerve-racking day, the moment of truth came. The head recruiter, a distinguished looking flight supervisor dressed in immaculate uniform, read out a list of names which included Elizabeth's. She then asked the people she had named to leave the room through a back door and wait outside. They were joined by one of the recruiters, a thin Asian lady, who looked at the group with a solemn expression.

'I have to tell you that you *have* been successful at this stage. Congratulations. Please don't cheer loudly as the others might hear you - they have not been successful on this occasion.'

The chosen few let out a collective gasp, and some even looked as though they were about to cry with happiness. Elizabeth had not seen any of them later, after the one-on-one interviews the following week.

Was it fate, or just good luck? she thought to herself, stroking her knees which were protruding from the bubbles, tensing her back and then slowly relaxing it again.

The very first task of the day had been to stand up in front of the whole group and introduce yourself with your name, and then give a few pieces of information about yourself: hobbies for example. Elizabeth calculated that the assessors would be looking for three main things at this stage.

The first was the ability to follow the instructions as given, which meant not starting with 'The reason I want to be cabin crew is...' as most of the others had done - that was not the question being asked. The second thing was appearance, and although Elizabeth had no prior experience as cabin crew, she was determined to look every bit the part, not only the clothes, hair and makeup, but by projecting confident body language. The third was to be upbeat and positive in what she said, just like in any job interview, but maybe more obviously in this case. She could see the team of assessors were taking lots of notes on their clipboards.

During the downtime in the assessment day, suspicious of plants in the applicants, she had not let her guard down for a second, and managed not to frown or get distracted throughout the entire process. She made cheerful small talk with the other applicants on her table during the coffee break. Elizabeth recalled a strikingly beautiful woman she had had a conversation with during that break. She was called Lisa.

Lisa's mother was a purser for a Scandinavian airline, her father was a retired pilot. Lisa had always been determined to follow in her mother's footsteps. Elizabeth wrapped herself in a fluffy towel and sat on the bed, touched by a twinge of sadness when she reflected that Lisa had not made the cut. It was possible that she had found a place in another airline by now, but it did not make the memory any less melancholy.

Sometimes you win, often you lose, she thought.

She flipped the channel over on the TV and caught the ending of Titanic dubbed in French.

Often you lose, but the important thing is not to give up.

Elizabeth took her time doing her hair and face, put on a chic black cocktail dress, switched off Céline, and went down to join her co-workers.

The whole crew had showed up including the captain and the first officer. In Elizabeth's experience, it was unusual for everyone to make it, but the flight over had been relatively free of problems, and as it turned out, Elizabeth was not the only newbie.

'Hi again,' Justin said.

'Hey, hi everyone,' Elizabeth said taking a seat at the long, marble bar and they returned the greeting. Behind the bar itself was a truly massive flatscreen TV showing a football match which the captain seemed to be half-watching.

'Let me get you a drink,' Justin offered.

'I'll just have an orange juice,' Elizabeth said. 'You look very different...'

'... in my civvies,' he finished.

'Yep,' she said.

'I've only been a first officer for eighteen months... despite appearances! I'm still getting used to seeing my colleagues morph downroute as well. I used to be a vet. Jane says you're new too?'

'Almost one year in,' Elizabeth said. 'So why the change?'

'Well, I suppose flying was always a hobby, I didn't really think about doing it as a job, and I just felt like after ten years working with animals, I fancied a change of scene, and I applied. Well, I got it,' he concluded. 'So... a year in, then?'

David started to sing *Like a Virgin* with a slurred voice.

'Wrong airline, princess,' Fiona quipped.

He squinted his eyes at her and mimed a cat scratching the air.

'You enjoying it?' Justin asked.

'I love it! I've never travelled so much before,' she replied. 'Sorry I didn't get a chance to pop into the flight deck, but we were so busy on the way over.'

'It's no problem at all. I suppose on a duty like this one, you guys just can't wait to land?'

'You bet. You could never get tired of a place like this,' Fiona said. 'Tomorrow we should go into town - you can get some real bargains here if you go outside the touristy bits.'

'Apparently Fiona here is an expert at haggling,' Jane said.

'Jane, you should come as well,' Fiona said.

'I have a bit of paperwork to do, but I might do. I can't stand being cooped up inside for too long.'

Matt had remained quiet.

'Hey, Matt, are you up for a group outing tomorrow, so to speak?' David asked, brandishing his champagne flute.

'Sure,' he replied. 'I need to look for a cheap pair of trainers actually, I'm just not sure if I'll be able to find them in my size.'

David winked discretely at Fiona and downed what was left of his champagne. He tapped on the empty glass.

'Right, the next round's on the captain!' he announced.

'What are we going to do with this one?' Tim said.

'So, who's up for breakfast on the beach?' Justin asked.

'I really fancy sleeping late,' Tim replied as David topped up his glass. Elizabeth noticed as he said that, that he had held eye contact with her the whole time. She blushed in spite of herself. Angela had a rule about pilots, but Elizabeth could not help but smile back.

They had put the captain in an enormous suite, Elizabeth noticed. Tim placed his hands firmly on Elizabeth's shoulders and leaned in to kiss her lips without hesitation. She was overwhelmed with the sudden intensity of the situation. His strong hands lifted her into his embrace and she responded with passion, acting on her instinct. She felt a distinct rub on her face from his stubble but did not draw back. She kept wondering if she was making a huge mistake by being there but tried to push the doubts to the back of her mind.

His hands moved down her body to her thighs. Their lips did not stop moving. She was impressed with his enthusiasm, and could already tell that this was a man who wanted to please his partner. She sided onto the bed and he kicked off his shoes and undid his shirt revealing a hairy chest. She beckoned him onto the bed. He stroked her sides and as she moved up close to him she could feel that he was excited. He stroked her hair back off her face and gave her deeper, slower kisses. She teased him with her tongue softly, then more aggressively, and he responded by moaning.

Things were moving fast, and he seemed to decide he needed to take it down a notch.

'Get on your front, I'm going to give you a massage,' he said, and she obeyed.

He unzipped the back of her cocktail dress and started to knead her shoulders and spine with his firm yet precise hands. She panted with pleasure.

'You like it?' he asked.

'Yes, don't stop, don't stop,' she begged.

He continued to massage her and worked his way ever lower.

She squealed as he gave her buttocks a playful spank.

'Sorry, I couldn't resist!'

She turned to face him and kissed him again, this time little pecks, first on the lips, then on his cheeks and forehead. His face wore a confident, experienced expression.

'Tim, do you have...?' she asked as delicately as possible.

'Always carry them with me,' he replied cheerfully.

'*I bet you do!*' she whispered.

Screw Angela's rules - Elizabeth wanted, in fact she needed pleasure, and she was sure it would be a pleasurable night.

After a minute of writhing on top of her his body seemed to freeze.

'Is everything okay?' she asked, shaking her head.

There was a long pause.

'That was fantastic,' he replied.

It took Elizabeth a few moments to realise.

'You... you've finished?' she asked in disbelief.

'Fantastic,' he groaned and rolled over onto his back

ready for sleep.

The night was over.

6

The next morning Elizabeth's phone buzzed and beeped on the bedside table. She came back to life, shivering. The air conditioner had overchilled her room.

Thank God I didn't drink last night, things went far enough teetotal, she thought, blinking rapidly at the alarm screen as memories from the night before returned. She filled the kettle with mineral water and put a peppermint teabag in a cup. The room phone rang and full clarity returned.

'Morning, honey. Bad news, I'm afraid. David can't come,' Fiona said. 'The little lush has a hangover, it was all that champagne. I think him and the captain were the last ones to leave. Are you still up for a trip off the beaten track?'

'I still am. You know the city quite well then?' she asked trying to keep her voice from betraying her anxieties.

'I do, I used to come here all the time. But nowadays my roster is all two and four sector days,' she moaned. 'Someone has to bloody get them.'

'Mhm, there-and-backs are really annoying,' she said, thinking back to her first month of flying without even a single nightstop. It had been a real ordeal, especially being 'green crew' and being formally observed on the early flights. She would get back to her house and fall asleep as soon as she got into bed which in the early days seemed to spin.

'It's a big comedown for a Concorde Girl. Have you been to Los Angeles yet?' Fiona asked.

'No, not yet.'

'I think it's the best trip we do, and you usually get some big names on the passenger list.'

'Cool,' Elizabeth said.

'Right, I'll leave you to kick butt in the gym, see you for breakfast by the beach around ten,' she said.

'See you at ten!'

* * *

The gym was ostentatiously huge and featured indoor palm trees, a view of the many tennis courts and two cheerful blue swimming pools, one inside and one outside. Once the momentum got going, Elizabeth jogged intensely for a solid thirty minutes on the treadmill and a familiar, pleasurable high kicked in. The other few guests in the gym faded away and she was lost in the trance of her blaring iPhone and the rhythmic bounce of her feet on the belt.

'Well, hello stranger!'

It was Tim, who else, standing there in a black polo shirt and small white shorts.

'Good morning, I see you didn't sleep late in the end?' Elizabeth asked with confidence.

'You look flustered. Come for breakfast in an hour?' he asked.

'I'm going for breakfast... and last night stays last night, or did you want to brag?' she asked. This half-prepared conversation came out as a lot more aggressive than she had intended, and Tim suddenly looked taken aback. She hoped she wasn't embarrassing him too much.

'Not that you would,' she added. 'I mean...'

'No, fair enough,' he replied. 'I want to have breakfast by the beach with you and the rest of the crew, and last night was just between us.'

She gave him a friendly smile.

'I think that's for the best, and I'm not naïve, it wouldn't be good for either of us to talk about it,' she said. 'These things can happen.'

Tim smiled back, nodded politely, and headed for the cross trainers.

7

Elizabeth picked up a replica Dolce & Gabbana handbag and felt its weight. It was white with black polka dots, and the quality was extremely good. She estimated that the real thing would easily cost over a thousand pounds back home. It was light and attractive, but inside there was still ample space to fit lots of things.

'It suits you, you should get it,' said Fiona.

'This one's nice, too,' suggested David, picking up a brown Valentino handbag with a silver chain that glimmered in the sun.

'It's a bit too rock 'n' roll for me, but it's an impressive fake,' she said. 'Nobody would ever be able to tell the difference,' she added.

'That's why I love this place,' Fiona philosophised. 'With fakes as good as this, why would you bother shelling out for the real thing?'

The souk was vast, and there was an extensive selection of goods on offer. Hanging up alongside the tables were clothes, souvenirs, books, CDs and even tools, garden and kitchen equipment and furniture. Many stands were offering snacks and fresh juices.

'Aha!' Elizabeth said, spotting an inflatable paddling pool hanging up at the next stall. She glided over and asked the young stall holder if she could take a look while David and Fiona continued to rummage through the bags and suitcases.

'Just 500 Dirhams, and it's top quality,' he informed her in perfect English.

The box looked new, but the brand was an unknown name.

'Take 300?' she asked.

'Three! But it's such *good* quality, suitable for adults and children, this will last for years, so unfortunately I can't take less than 500. Less than 500, I simply cannot accept,' he added, frowning theatrically.

'Take 350, final offer,' Elizabeth said, and paused to hold her ground.

Silently the boy took out a large carrier bag and transferred the pool into it.

'Enjoy,' he said counting out the notes with glee.

'That's about twenty-five quid, I hope it actually works,' said David when she rejoined the pair at the luggage stall.

'I feel so bad haggling,' Elizabeth groaned.

'But it's expected, darling, you'll get the hang of it,' said Fiona. 'You just got yourself a bargain, at least in English prices.'

'Yeah,' she said, 'Angela is going to be happy now she has an excuse to strut around in a wet bikini. Do either of you know Angela, she started at the same time as me?'

'Is that Angela Eastfield? Do you live with her?' David asked.

'Yes, that's right,' Elizabeth replied.

'We had a five day Tehran together last month, she's lovely,' he said.

'It's nice to have some fresh faces around,' Fiona added. 'It was a long time before they took on new crew.'

The trio walked on and came to a stop at a book stand. There were titles in many languages, but most of the books were either Arabic or English bestsellers. Unlike most of the other places Elizabeth had seen so far, the prices were clearly labelled and she worked out that the books were very cheap. One oldish book seemed to stand out to her - it was by an agony aunt she did not recognize, Judith. It was a compilation of people's letters to a problem page over the years. She flicked through the crinkly pages.

'Time for a cup of tea?' David asked.

'Yes, let's have a sit down and chill out for a bit, it's getting seriously hot now,' Fiona replied.

Elizabeth paid for the book and they headed towards a huge open-air food court at the very edge of the market which was not so busy. Away from the crowds, there were some stray cats running around. In her head, Elizabeth wrote an imaginary letter to the agony aunt.

Dear Judith,

I'm worried that my life is not really going anywhere. You see, the men I attract are only really after one thing, and I feel as though I should be settling down soon.

The problem is, I'm probably still too young to start a family, and even if I did, I'd worry that I was missing out. A psychic in town told me to look out for a person 'of great vision' who would lead me to my destiny, but should I trust someone who is probably just a charlatan, making up vague predictions to cash in on a succession of desperate saps?

How pathetic she sounded to herself. What had brought on this dissatisfaction? The letdown with the captain? Her failed relationships in the past? She wondered why she had let Tim chat her up so quickly. Maybe it was a lack of goals to go for since securing the job. Was it even a job she should take seriously as a career? *Nobody enjoys being directionless for very long*, she thought to herself.

'I am SO hungover,' David moaned.

'So no clubs tonight?' Elizabeth asked.

'I'll have to see how I feel,' he said, and she patted his shoulder in sympathy.

Fiona took out a blue box of Camel cigarettes, and asked the waitress for three Arabic coffees with sugar.

'You're going to love this,' she said to Elizabeth. 'I'm not really that hungry, though, I think I'll leave off having food until later.'

The breakfast had been long, but uneventful. Tim had kept his word and acted with discretion, in fact he had almost behaved as though Elizabeth had not been there, and the whole crew with the exception of an absent Matt had had a first class feast.

In contrast to the noise and crowds in the rest of the souk, this area was calm, full of large parasols and soft jazz piping through. Elizabeth exhaled and nestled into her seat - a sturdy plastic beach chair with a small, ornate cushion. The paddling pool got its own chair.

Some old men wearing traditional dress were smoking shisha pipes peacefully, a pair of them playing chess, and she noticed that a few tourists, mainly couples, were relaxing here, too. Faintly, in the background, she could hear the call to prayer starting.

'What are your next trips? I've just got a Dublin standover - two of them in a row,' David said.

'Just there-and-backs for a while,' Fiona groaned.

'I have a Tel Aviv and a Bishkek soon,' Elizabeth offered.

'Bishkek, lucky thing. I love it over there,' David said. 'Want to swap?'

'I've never been, so I think I'm going to keep it this time. Sorry,' she said.

'Shame, it's a beautiful place this time of year, if you can stand that length of flight. It's ten hours on your feet.'

'Don't listen to him, it's nothing!' Fiona said. 'You normally get a lot of people who just want to sleep through, so it's not much work at all.'

'True,' he said, 'but when you're tired it's a tough gig. Time zones. Jet lag.'

A group of women selling pink and yellow flowers crossed through the courtyard, and the heat of the powerful sun bore down despite the large canvas parasols. The waitress brought over a tray with a gold coffee pot and some glasses, three tiny cups and a large bottle of San Pellegrino. Elizabeth poured herself some water, and discovered that, thankfully, it was ice cold.

'I'm planning on having a nice little siesta when I get back to my room,' Fiona said.

'Good plan,' said David. 'It's a shame the others couldn't come, but maybe Matt will be up for later,' he added, perking up.

'You're all over Matt, aren't you?!' said Fiona, blowing smoke upwards into the air and leaning back into her seat. 'He's probably got a girlfriend. Do you want me to find out?'

'Are you a betting woman?' he asked.

'Oh we can't do that, but I'm sure I'm right,' she said.

It occurred to Elizabeth that Matt had not been quiet because that was his usual personality, but she sensed that something else was going on in his life. There was something troubling him, and a sense of curiosity about him started to develop.

'Didn't he say he wanted some trainers last night?' she asked.

'Babe, I can't remember anything about last night, I need to stop drinking,' David said.

But Elizabeth could remember the previous night, and now wished she had reined in her impulses. Although there would be no awkwardness - she now knew she could rely on Tim to keep quiet - it seemed after the fact that the whole thing had merely been another unsuccessful attempt to reach a sense of fulfillment that would simply go on eluding her, and she felt certain that would still be the case even if it had lasted more than ten minutes.

She lifted the tiny cup to her lips and sipped her coffee. It was sweet, strong, and tasted like cardamom. It relaxed her slightly.

'Good, isn't it?' asked Fiona.

'It's absolutely delicious,' she agreed, 'I'll have to get some to take home,' and she soon finished the special cup and poured herself seconds of the steaming, thick concoction.

After their rest, Elizabeth and her two colleagues picked up their shopping bags and made their way back into the market. Fiona stopped to look at some colourful rugs and the stall owner was excitedly explaining what made them so special, including the history of the rugs and their cultural significance while she smiled politely, nodding now and then when suddenly Elizabeth felt a sharp pain in her left calf and dropped the paddling pool.

She looked down in horror. A stray cat had scratched her leg and run straight off.

'Oh my God, Liz, are you okay?' David screamed. 'That cat came out of nowhere!'

Elizabeth was speechless and simply stood there, staring down at the red patch surrounding the fresh hole in her jeans.

8

Back in her hotel room, Elizabeth glanced down at the long scratch marks on her leg. It was not serious, but there was a substantial amount of blood that had soaked through the jeans. She stumbled over from the doorway to the bathroom and ran the cold tap. In the minibar there was a miniature Smirnoff. She took the vodka and poured a little on a pad fashioned from toilet paper.

She washed the wound using a facecloth and dabbed on some vodka, wincing at the sting. She washed her hands and dried them on a towel leaving the trouser leg rolled up to air the cuts. She sat down at the desk and calmed down. After a few moments she took out some Royal Maluf writing paper from the drawer.

Tim, I hope you're enjoying the trip. Do you want to come over to my room later for a quick chat? I'm in 512.

- Elizabeth.

It was after three o'clock and she was getting hungry. She picked up her key card and walked down to the end of the corridor to the captain's suite, bent down and slipped the note under the door. Inside she could hear a muffled groan which stopped abruptly. Then the door clicked and swept open.

Tim stood there in a hotel dressing gown looking sweaty and red, his hairy legs exposed below the end of the gown.

'Elizabeth?' he said, slightly out of breath.

'I just wanted to leave a note, if you're free later on...' she started. She picked up the unmistakable scent of perfume in the air.

'You're not alone,' she said.

'I'm a bit busy right now, but I'll give you a ring later, sorry about all this,' he explained.

From the corner of her eye, Elizabeth thought she could make out a figure in the room - was it a nude woman standing with a drink? Her heart started to beat quickly and she looked down.

'Okay,' she said, starting to walk backwards.

'You've hurt your leg,' he said, noticing the cut underneath her turned up jeans.

'It's nothing, just a scratch,' she replied, beginning to walk away.

'I'll give you a call later on, yeah?' he said.

The door closed slowly and she headed back to her room dazed. It was not that he had actually done anything wrong, but Elizabeth felt embarrassed about the note, and as she went back into her room, she imagined she could hear a female voice coming from the suite.

She sat on the bed and her face burned. As her thoughts raced, in spite of herself, she began to cry warm, heavy tears. Tim really *was* enjoying the trip, and it occurred to her that she might just be another silly conquest to him, perhaps just like the woman he was hosting right now - another notch on the bedpost.

She really had just wanted a quick chat, it was as innocent as that. She was in no desperate need of a repeat performance and doubted she ever would be, yet the sense of rejection and most of all embarrassment stung all the same. It looked so desperate, and what if someone had happened to see her? She picked up the remote control and turned on the TV to drown out the sounds of her little sobs. She spread out onto the bed, and hugging a pillow she began to nap.

The sun had begun to set when she woke up. The TV was still on. An old black and white Arabic film was showing, and for a few moments Elizabeth watched the screen passively, not understanding a word, but not thinking of changing the channel. She got up and opened the window. From the balcony she saw people walking along the reddish beach and could smell that somewhere down below people were barbecuing meat and fish. A pang of hunger clenched her stomach.

She rolled over to the bedside table and snatched the room service menu from its plastic holder. She decided to go simple - some hummus and chips with a side salad. Luckily the cuts were already looking as though they were starting to heal, and with food on the way, she started to cheer up. There was a soft knock at the door.

'Just me,' said a male voice. Elizabeth looked through the spy hole. It was David.

'Hey,' she said, and pulled open the door.

'Is your leg okay?' he asked as he came into the room.

'Yeah, it's fine. I've just ordered some chips and stuff if you want some?' she asked.

'Good idea, I haven't had anything solid since breakfast except some aspirin. So have you tried out the pool?' he asked.

Elizabeth smiled.

'I've just had a nap... Actually, quite a long nap. What time is it anyway?' she asked.

'Coming up to nine,' he replied, looking at his watch.

'Nine! It's so late, I didn't realise how tired I was.'

'We *were* walking around all morning, I was pretty shattered as well. I'm feeling a lot better now, though. I've been drinking lots of juice and I did my yoga.'

'You do yoga?' Elizabeth asked as they walked over to the balcony and she pulled around a seat for him.

'I've been going to yoga classes regularly for three years. Does that surprise you?' he asked.

'You just seemed a bit... cynical,' she said.

'You had me all wrong!' David replied and laughed. 'Someone's having a barbecue,' he said.

'Yes, it's made me ravenous.'

'Are you okay, though? You look a bit flustered.'

Elizabeth thought back to her encounter with Tim earlier. What had she expected? What had she honestly wanted to 'chat' about? Now it seemed obvious that she had done exactly the wrong thing, and if anything she had only stroked his ego. Now she imagined him as she thought he might see himself: a womaniser, a man in a well-paid position playing at being a playboy whenever the mood took him.

'I'm fine, I just think the heat is getting to me,' she replied.

'You're going to love Bishkek,' he said. 'It never gets too hot, and there are parks everywhere, you feel like you're surrounded by nature.'

'Do they ogle at women like they do over here?' she asked.

'It's completely different, I wouldn't worry about being stared at,' he said. 'What on Earth are you watching?' he asked.

A song had started on the TV - it must have been a musical.

'No idea, it was just on, something Moroccan, I guess.'

'When did you order the room service?' he asked.

'Not that long ago. You should stay and have some with me.'

'Oh dear, she's on the vodka,' David said, noticing the miniature on the side.

'No, that was for my leg, honestly!' Elizabeth replied.

'Mhm, your leg. I love Smirnoff and coke. Let's ask the room service to bring up some drinks,' he said.

'Go ahead, it's quite reasonable here even before the discount. I'll have some Cinzano,' she said.

'Cinzano - get you! No gym for you tomorrow, then. Shall we invite the others?' he asked.

'I wasn't expecting a room party, but it would be nice to see Fiona,' she said. 'She was so sweet earlier, showing us where to find the bargains.'

David picked up the phone and dialed.

'Room party in 512, we're expecting you, and bring along a bottle, you old tart,' he said flippantly. 'I got the answering machine, she's probably getting her nails or hair done.'

He picked up the receiver again to order the drinks and some snacks. Elizabeth smiled and thought to herself how ridiculous she was being: apart from the cat, this trip was turning out to be one of the most pleasant she had been on since starting at the airline, so why get upset about an idiotic captain who she had spent a very brief time with? It was just that she had not wanted it to be hurried, it should have been exciting and hedonistic. And with these thoughts, a sense of unease returned.

9

Angela was in the crew room and skipped over to see her friend.

'Hey, honey, how was the trip?' she asked.

'It was great, but I hurt my leg,' Elizabeth replied. 'There was a street cat that took a disliking to me in the market.'

'That's weird, what happened?' Angela asked.

'I was just standing there looking at some rugs, and a stray scratched me. Then it ran off,' she said.

'Are you okay?' Angela asked looking baffled.

'Yes, I'm fine, it's healing nicely. How about you? Where are you off to?' she asked.

'Hopefully anywhere, and soon. I'm on airport standby. I've been hanging around this dump for three hours, I just want someone to shoot me. I'm bored out of my mind.' She lifted up the tiny Nokia to show Elizabeth.

'Three hours, that's pretty harsh. I guess nobody's called in sick, then.'

'I've been looking at the departures board, and there are some nice destinations coming up. I'd take a weekend in Paris if I had the choice,' she said. 'I'd even be happy to get a Moscow there-and-back at this stage if I'm honest, it's better than just doing NOTHING.'

'Hang in there, you might get lucky. I'm shattered, I really need to get back to the house and sleep,' Elizabeth said, and yawned.

'Okay, babes, get some rest, and if I don't get called, I'll see you later on.'

At that point, Angela noticed Matt walking through the crew lounge towards the printers. Matt smiled and made a half-wave at Elizabeth.

'Who is *he*?' Angela asked, a broad grin on her face.

'That's Matt, he was with us in Agadir. He's a pretty quiet guy.'

'He's gorgeous!' Angela enthused.

'He keeps himself to himself.'

'Tall, handsome, broad shoulders... he's probably gay, such a shame.'

'To be honest with you, I have no idea. He didn't go out with us downroute. It's anyone's guess.'

'Right, I'll let you head off. I'm going to read the newspaper. Again.'

'Oh, I meant to tell you, I managed to get a paddling pool in Agadir, I just hope it works,' she said.

'Great! How much was it, let me give you half.'

'Nope, not telling, you don't have to give me anything.'

'You're too kind, dear,' Angela said, tilting her head.

'Right, then. See you later, maybe?'

'Yep, safe journey home,' Angela said as she walked off in the same direction as Matt.

The Tube journey took about fifteen minutes as Elizabeth lived very near to the airport, and as she headed back to her houseshare, she smiled to think how surprising it could still be to experience a sort of reverse culture shock. The English signs and the appearance of the houses struck her as so exaggeratedly British in comparison with the things she had encountered over the last three days during the trip. London was experiencing a heatwave, and her uniform was beginning to feel uncomfortably tight and warm. Inside the carriage it was hotter than it had been in Morocco.

A tourist stood aside as Elizabeth got off the train, pulling her case behind her. The air on the platform was hot and dry, and Elizabeth walked slowly, with poise, up to the exit gates. Outside the station a car boot sale was in full swing. She walked past. Although she was thirsty, she did not feel willing to go into the supermarket across the road in full uniform with a suitcase. She was in the habit of removing her name badge as soon as she left the airport in a bid to achieve anonymity.

It was only a five minute walk to the house, but today it seemed much longer. She could not wait to kick off her shoes, get out of the uniform and relax in the garden.

She unlocked her front door and went straight into the kitchen to pour herself a drink.

'Hi, how are you?' asked Paul, closing the oven.

'Hey, Paul, I'm great. Tired, but fine. And you?' she asked.

Paul smiled and nodded.

'I have to tell you one important thing,' he said. 'Tonight I will have a party in the house and garden. I hope this is not a problem?' he asked.

'Of course not. It's your house as well, I hope you feel at home now,' she said.

'You are invited, of course,' he added. 'It's just some people from work and I think some of their girlfriends,' he said. 'We will use the garden and make barbecue.'

'That's fine with me,' Elizabeth said.

'What is wrong with your leg?' he asked, noticing the bright blue plasters.

'Nothing much, just a scratch,' she replied. 'Nothing to worry about.'

In her room she unpacked her mobile from her stuffed handbag. This time, luckily, it had remained switched off and there was a full battery. She sent a text message to her dad to say that she wanted to keep her old clothes and CDs, the rest could go into boxes or be safely thrown away. Then she sent a message to Angela to tell her she needed to have a talk. She thought again about Tim, but then her thoughts switched to Matt.

The reaction he had provoked in Angela was strange - although he was objectively a good looking young man, he had not immediately caught Elizabeth's attention. Perhaps that was because he was a work colleague in a different sense from the pilots, and she had unconsciously avoided going through the curtain on the flight back to London. As for pilots, Angela's rule was to avoid them like the plague. There was a power dynamic that she claimed would make for an impossible fit.

You would be putting yourself into a position where they

could lord it over you as a superior. However, it *was* often the case that marriages took place between pilots and stewardesses, that much was clear from everything Elizabeth had heard. In fact, whole families existed with generations in the aviation industry. *It must be an especially difficult relationship to maintain*, she thought, the difficulty being that the husband and wife were constantly travelling, so when would they find any time to spend together?

In her ideal future, there was a loving husband: a modern man... definitely one who knew how to cook and do housework and share responsibility for their two, or maybe three, beloved children. Romantic nights in front of the TV with a film on, romantic meals out in restaurants with soft lighting and flowers. In her vision of the future she could imagine herself as not that much different from now, a little older and wiser perhaps, but who was in the male role? A man with vision, the psychic had predicted. What did that even mean? It had occurred to her that he might have even been making a crafty, concealed advance since he was a 'clairvoyant'.

There was a knock on her door.

'Elizabeth, do you want some Polish cake?' Paul asked.

The cinnamon-like smell of what he had been baking was delicious. Elizabeth chuckled at the coincidence.

'Thanks for the offer, Paul, but I'm totally full. What time are your friends coming over?'

'Not long, they will come soon,' he replied.

'Do you need a hand getting things ready?' she asked through the door.

'I'm sorry?'

'Can I help you take out drinks to the garden?'

'It is all ready, thank you,' came the reply.

'Cool,' she said, and Paul shuffled back down the stairs.

Elizabeth started up her laptop and checked her e-mail. Just junk. Her phone buzzed. Two new messages came through.

'No worries, take care, love. Dad x.'

The second message was a text from an unknown number.

It's Tim. Got your number from the crew list. I want to have that chat and explain what happened in Agadir. Sorry if I upset you.

She decided to delete it and pretend she had never received it, pushing any second thoughts from her mind. If she did ever fly with him again and he asked, she could just say she had never received it. She breathed out slowly.

Downstairs heavy metal started on the stereo.

10

'You did what?' Angela asked.

She was livid that she had not been called for a duty after five and a half hours of waiting around at Heathrow.

'It was supposed to be a one off, a bit of fun. But I feel a bit like I've been used.'

'What did I tell you? They're all the same, I don't trust any of them. You should never give them what they want. Put it down to experience.'

'The problem is, that night, in that frame of mind, I was *ready* to enjoy it. Not... that... it was any good.'

'Well what were you expecting?' Angela asked.

'That he would know what to do, I suppose,' Elizabeth tried to explain.

'Well it's not rocket science! Please tell me you used protection,' she said in exasperation.

'Well it's more of an *art* than a science. And of course I'm not like that. I mean, I'm impulsive but not I'm not deranged,' she said.

'Then he must *not* have had a lot of practice by the sounds of it.'

'Hm. Well, that's the other problem. The next day...'

She went on to explain what she had seen, or rather what she thought she had seen in Tim's suite after slipping the note under his door.

'What a bastard!' Angela scowled.

'How was he supposed to know I'd turn up with a note?' Elizabeth asked.

'You're defending him. He's obviously having a mid-life crisis and you just pandered to it,' Angela said, shaking her head.

'He's only in his late thirties, if that.'

'Ugh, young captains are the worst - the worst! I can't stand the arrogance,' she uttered with pure scorn.

'Well he texted me after the flight back. I deleted it,' she said.

'Saying what?'

'He wants to talk.'

'And you deleted it, good. Forget him. You just need to hope he's not rostered for any more of your trips any time soon.' She took off her jacket and stretched out her arms. 'And pray he keeps quiet about it, not that he will.'

'Oh, you don't think...' Elizabeth started.

'Honey, you need to wake up. Just wake up. He can brag about bagging you downroute, and the worst thing is it'll be true,' she said.

A short silence followed.

'You're right,' Elizabeth sighed. 'Who do you think the woman in the room was?'

'Who knows? Maybe a whore, they're all at it.'

'A prostitute? I don't think he's the type who'd need to...'

'Trust me, babe, he's exactly the type. Insatiable.'

'Insatiable,' Elizabeth repeated.

'Do what I said, put it down to experience. If you hear anything, deny it. Don't give him the satisfaction. He enjoyed himself? Great, but now it's time to get serious. No more captains, no more first officers,' she said.

'I didn't sleep with any first officers,' Elizabeth said sadly.

'Good, keep it that way,' Angela replied. 'Now give me a hug.'

Downstairs the party was in full swing.

'Are you in the mood?' Angela asked.

'Not really, what kind of people has he got over?'

'They're all engineers, all young engineers.'

'How young?'

They both began to giggle.

'By the way, did you have a guy called David on your last Tel Aviv crew? David Jones? He said he'd met you,' Elizabeth asked.

'Yeah, he's so sweet. He took us to this bar called Evita, it was a lots of fun.'

'He was in Agadir with me. Did you know he does yoga?' she asked

'He didn't strike me as the type, but you never know, do you? Come on, let's go and socialise.'

As an afterthought, Angela added, 'By the way, I got talking to that Matt. We might have a date soon. Not an official date, but a meet up outside of work, so... Mystery solved!'

'Angela, you don't waste any time!' Elizabeth teased as they went downstairs.

'Says you!' she replied.

Paul's taste in music was eclectic. When Angela and Elizabeth went into the garden an old Take That song was playing loudly replacing the rock from earlier, and there was a handful of guests sitting around enjoying the ambiance, chatting, a couple of others danced awkwardly.

Paul offered Elizabeth and Angela drinks and started preparing the barbecue. She noticed that the garden bin was already nearly full of empty beer and cider cans.

'Hi, I'm Nicko, I'm from Amsterdam' the man said.

'Hi, I'm Angela, but you can call me Ange! I'm from Surrey. This is Elizabeth, another of the housemates,' she said grinning.

'Nice to meet you,' Nicko said. He was tall, thin, and had a sensible, short haircut.

'You must be a pilot,' Angela said.

'Is it so obvious?' he asked.

'Yes, but nobody's perfect. Sit with us. Are you over here in London on a trip?' she asked.

'No, I'm over here to do some sim training, nothing exciting but at least I get to see some of London. Good weather. Nice time to be here. Are you both cabin crew?' he asked, trying to get Elizabeth back into the conversation, but in reality she was not really up for socialising, and it seemed like Angela had already pounced in spite of the rules she had been laying down only minutes before.

Paul sat beside her with a can of Pepsi taking a break from barbecuing as Nicko and Angela became engrossed in their smalltalk.

'You seem a bit sad,' he said.

Elizabeth smiled.

'No big deal. What are you cooking?'

'Just some chicken and minted lamb kebabs. You will have some?' he said.

'I'm on a diet at the moment, but we'll see. Maybe later,' she said.

'Great. I haven't had much time to talk to you since I moved in,' he said.

'Yes, I'm sorry about that. I've been... Well, you know we're always flying around the world, that's just the nature of the job,' she said.

It occurred to her that she most likely was coming across as a little dull or bored, and she didn't want to.

'You have good taste in music,' she said.

'Thank you!' Paul said. 'I always thought there isn't any

point listening to this genre or that genre, there is only good music and bad music,' he said.

'I totally agree. When I was growing up my mother never stopped playing the piano, so I got a whole mix of stuff.'

'That's fantastic,' Paul said.

Every now and then Angela let out a huge burst of laughter.

'She's enjoying the party,' Paul said.

'Certainly is,' Elizabeth said.

Angela stood up to excuse herself, she 'needed the ladies'. She asked Elizabeth to join her. In the corridor she stopped and looked serious for a second.

'What's wrong?' Elizabeth asked.

'I got a text from Matt, the guy from your crew,' she said.

'Already?' she asked. 'It's moving fast!'

'Yes, I got his number! And he wants a date. He used that word. I just wanted to check if that, well it's a concrete thing now, just... if that was... okay?'

'Why wouldn't it be okay?' she asked.

'Well, you met him first. And he's, you know... He's cute,' she said.

'You can date whoever you want. And clearly will,' she added gesturing to the garden.

'That guy, Nicko, he's very... Amusing. He's a funny guy, but come on, that's a pilot,' she explained.

'From a totally different airline,' Elizabeth whispered smiling.

'Yeah. A lot to think about,' Angela replied.

Elizabeth laughed.

'Do what you like, I'm sure both Nicko and Matt would be happy to date you,' she said.

'Thanks, Elizabeth,' Angela said and gave her a peck on the cheek. 'You're a true mate,' she added.

11

It was the morning after the barbecue, and Elizabeth woke up prematurely. The sun had risen a few hours before and the room was hot. She got out of the bed and opened a window. The slow, piercing roar of aircraft coming in to land cut through the sound of a deep voice below. Paul was in the garden speaking to someone on the phone in Polish. Her first thoughts were that after Bishkek, there would be a lot of things to go over and memorise before the recurrent, and it would be best to start organising her revision notes in advance. The feeling of being underprepared was all too familiar. She began to recall one of her earliest flights that had started with a nightmarish briefing and just got worse from then on.

Donald West - how could she forget that name? Donald was known by everyone in the airline for being a perfectionist - although often more offensive epithets were employed. He was an older cabin service manager who relished making his subordinates' lives a misery. He achieved this through a combination of over-the-top briefings, which were more like interrogations, and his numerous unnecessary reports. Donald was fastidious with people as directly as he wished, and had a fetish for bureaucracy.

It had been an overnight trip to Manchester with minimum rest, a particularly unappetising piece of rostering, but Elizabeth had arrived fresh-faced and early when she swiped in that night. Donald was already in the briefing room sitting down with a huge suitcase on the floor beside him, a leather folder and a pile of print-outs on his lap.

'Hi, I'm Elizabeth.'

No reply. As he sized her up, the other two crew members, a tall blonde lady called Jessica and a stout, smiley man called Owen arrived.

'Right, now we're all here, let's kick off with an easy one. We're in the air and we experience explosive decompression. What is your first action?' He turned to Elizabeth.

'My first action is to sit down and put a seatbelt on,' she said.

Silence.

'... And put an oxygen mask on,' she added.

'Correct,' Donald said with a frown.

'Elizabeth, in all the chaos, you burned your arm badly on the tea. After running it under the cold water from the spigot for the recommended five full minutes, you dressed it with a burns shield. What two kinds of medicine do we have in the first aid kit for pain relief?'

'Paracetamol,' she said.

'And?'

A long silence followed. Elizabeth's face flushed, her mind was blank.

'And?!' he demanded, visibly annoyed.

'Ibuprofen?' she guessed.

'There is no ibuprofen in the first aid kit, and this is basic knowledge.'

'Aspirin?' Owen chimed in.

'That is correct,' snapped Donald. 'What else do we use aspirin for? Jessica?'

'Heart attacks on the advice of Med Link,' she recited.

'Good.'

The briefing, or rather the grilling went on in the same way for over fifteen minutes, and as Donald continued, the sense of dread rose inside Elizabeth. She knew that this was his way of going about his job, it being unimportant in the grand scheme of things, a way of operating that offered him a sensation of power over others, but she had no choice but to go along with his performance. Could anyone really take things this seriously?

The flight took off. Given the supervisor, it was no surprise that Elizabeth was left with the position in business class. She would have to work right alongside Donald, and true to form he nitpicked during the entire brief flight. Elizabeth could do nothing right.

'You need to read up on service standards as well as the health and safety information that should already be familiar to you. I'm not confident you know what you're doing at all, in fact you're lucky I didn't offload you at Heathrow,' he told her when they took their seats for landing. At no point could Elizabeth relax.

The crew checked into the hotel, however the pilots were staying at another hotel further away from Manchester Airport. It had taken Elizabeth by surprise that Donald had been acting like old chums with the captain and the first officer in stark contrast to the cabin crew.

'Don't take any notice of him,' said Owen in the lobby as soon as Donald was out of sight. 'He's known for this kind of crap, even on a good day. He's constantly on a power trip.'

'So it's not just me, then?' she asked.

'God, no,' said Jessica. 'Actually I'm surprised you haven't come across his name already, he's the worst by far. I had a Cairo there-and-back with him last year, which is a nightmare in itself, and he made us all spend the entire turnaround reading our manuals because we didn't know about the Tokyo Convention.'

'The what?'

'The rules about laws changing when the doors are open, that stuff. He's so... extra.'

Elizabeth laughed politely as Donald walked from the toilet to the front of the reception desk.

'What's so funny?' he snapped, his face expressionless.

'We were just talking about our initial training,' said Owen.

'A hazy memory to some of you, apparently. Right. I'm going to get my six hours' sleep. When we get back to Heathrow I think you should all know in advance that there is going to be a debriefing. I'm not happy with the flight up here, and by the look of it neither were the passengers.'

With that, he turned and strutted off, his suitcase in tow.

'It's full of manuals,' Owen said in a stage whisper.

Elizabeth did not dare laugh, even politely. She was

already seriously worried about the debriefing.

'Hey, don't panic,' said Jessica. 'The Wicked Witch of the West always does this kind of thing. I'd be more worried if he *didn't* debrief us and threaten to talk to managers.'

'So he won't? Speak to my line manager I mean?' she asked.

'And say what? You're still new, it's going to take time before you can recite the entire contents of the first aid kit, or answer all of the typical briefing questions.' She gave Elizabeth a hug.

'And non-typical ones,' added Owen.

'It's been so stressful for a half-hour flight,' Elizabeth said quietly.

'Don't worry, we're halfway through now. I was dreading this little trip, too. But if you have his name on your roster, nobody will swap with you,' said Owen. 'If all else fails, throw your bottle of water over him, he might melt.'

* * *

She took out her big blue ringbinder, the one holding the main manual, leafed through the thick first aid section and sighed. Even after twelve months, this stuff was still tough. The main problem was that the supervisors tended to always ask the same old briefing questions. For instance the firefighting procedure came up at least half of the time. That meant a lot of material was never covered. Elizabeth put on a T-shirt and her silk gown and went down to the garden.

The barbecue now looked old and used, the bricks blackened heavily despite it being a relatively new addition to the garden.

'Good morning,' said Paul. 'Very early.'

'Morning. Is Angela up yet?' she asked

'No. Actually I did not sleep, I was awake the whole night,' he said. 'I have a bunch of tests coming soon and I have not given up much time for study.'

'That makes two of us, I'm still at the stage of planning for how I'm going to organise my notes,' she said. 'Organising the organisation, planning to plan...'

Paul nodded wisely and said, 'we will get there. In the end we will get there.'

12

Matt sat in a noisy McDonald's packed with early evening customers opposite Angela devouring his spicy veg wrap. The vigour reminded her of a lion relishing its prey.

'Are you a vegetarian?' Angela asked.

'Nope, I just don't trust the meat at places like this. I used to work at a Burger King after I left school,' he said.

'I'm sure it's fine. Anyway, whose idea was it to come here? I'm not really a fast food kind of person.'

'Ha, I thought it would be good to go somewhere cheap. I'm trying to save money.'

'I see, and what are you saving up for, if I may ask?'

'I've set my sights on this,' he said, pulling out his phone.

'A motorbike?' Angela asked.

'This is not just any old motorbike. It's a Yamaha YBR125.'

'Cool. What's so special about it?'

'Well, it has a 4-stroke, fuel injected engine, a diamond-shaped chassis, 5-spoke cast alloy wheels...'

'It's like you're speaking another language!'

'Let's just say, it's expensive, but well worth it,' he explained.

'Do you drive as well, or just use a motorbike?' Angela

asked.

'No, I come to work in a car. An old banger, if you must know.'

Angela looked down. She had not meant to embarrass Matt, she knew roughly how much he made: like hers, it was not a salary worth writing home about.

'So, do you always want to fly, or do you have something else you're thinking about doing?' she asked.

'Well, I'm really into photography. That was one of the reasons I went for this job - so I could travel and take pictures. Apart from my passion for customer service,' he added.

They both laughed.

'What kind of photography?' Angela asked.

'Well I'm just as much into the technical side, but I've been told I have an artistic eye. I like to take photos of any subject pretty much. Buildings, nature, people...'

'Cool. Anything I can see?' she asked.

'Sure.'

He showed her a few snaps on his phone.

'They're really good, Matt,' Angela said, 'not that I know anything about art. Do you *take* them on your phone?'

'Never, no. I use proper equipment. Another expense. All these expensive hobbies.'

There was a pause.

'Do you want some of my chips? I'm not really supposed

to be eating this kind of thing,' Angela said.

'Sure, if you don't mind. I'm starving,' said Matt, opening another ketchup dip.

'So, what do you suggest we do after this? Something for the budget-conscious,' she said.

'Do you fancy doing some window shopping? I still need new trainers, actually, I've been meaning to buy a pair for weeks.'

He poked out a foot from under the table to show Angela one of his greying Pumas.

'Gross,' she said.

Angela could not help noticing the size of Matt's foot. He insisted on tidying away the used packaging neatly and putting it into the bin himself after the meal.

'You get used to doing that kind of thing at work and you can't switch off, can you? You're new, but you'll soon see,' Matt said, opening the door for her.

'No, I know exactly what you mean. At Halloween I gave some sweets to a group of kids who knocked at our door and when they left I told them to enjoy their flight.'

'Exactly!' he beamed. 'It's like a kind of brainwashing. Sometimes I feel like a robot.'

'Well, you can dream about doing something creative, like becoming a photographer. Some of us have no other talents at our disposal,' she said.

'Aw, don't say that, I'm sure you're good at lots of things,' he said in earnest.

'It doesn't seem to be the case. You might feel like a robot, but a lot of the time I feel like a kind of life size Barbie doll, and that's much worse.'

'What was your best subject at school?' he asked.

'Probably drama,' she said.

'Did you perform in any plays?' he asked.

'I was Lady Macbeth, but we were fourteen,' she said.

'Did you ever think about going into acting?' he asked. 'You have a very expressive face.'

'I'll take that as a compliment! Acting is probably a lot easier than what we do.'

They came to a halt at a jewellery shop and looked in at the Rolexes on display in the window.

'Beautiful,' Angela said.

'You'd have to save for a long time to get one of those,' Matt said.

'A very long time. Or you could just steal one,' she joked.

They walked on towards Fopp and went inside to look at DVDs. Matt picked up *Coming to America* and smiled.

'Cheesy,' Angela commented.

'What kind of films do you like?' he asked her.

Angela picked up *Clueless*.

'I'm a glamour girl,' she said blinking rapidly. They

walked upstairs to the CDs.

'I used to love her,' Angela said, holding up a bright pink Lil' Kim CD.

'Seriously? I would never have guessed you were into rap,' Matt said.

'Seriously, I have to buy it!' she said.

'Are your housemates going to be happy? It's slightly graphic, isn't it?' he asked with sarcasm.

'I'm sure Elizabeth would love Kim if she let her hair down a bit. She's been quite stressed lately, I don't know if you picked up on that.'

'It must be the recurrent, it's her first one, isn't it?' he asked.

'Yes, mine too, but there seems to be something else. It's like... she's never satisfied.'

'She's enjoying flying isn't she?' Matt asked.

'We both are, but I don't know, something's not right,' she replied.

It was becoming noisy and hot in the shop, so Angela paid for the CD and they continued walking.

'Let's go up to Selfridges,' Angela said.

13

The following day as Elizabeth was starting to study her manual in her room, Angela opened the door and slid inside.

'I've swapped onto your Tel Aviv,' she stated.

'That's great news, we should go out! Do the whole tourist thing,' Elizabeth said.

'You bet. It's going to be nice to have someone I know on a trip for a change.'

'Exactly, Angela. I don't want to just sit on the beach, though.'

'I got a guide book at the airport.'

'Cool. What happened to *Men Love Bitches*?' Elizabeth asked.

Angela folded her arms.

'That book didn't tell me anything I hadn't already mastered years ago,' she replied.

'The expert!' Elizabeth laughed. 'Seriously, though, self-help books - a waste of time.'

'Cheaper than visiting psychics,' Angela replied.

'Yeah, I wasn't really impressed, but the things he said have been playing on my mind.'

'The things he said could apply to anyone, it's called cold-reading, it's just a load of vague crap,' Angela said.

'But still...' Elizabeth started.

'At least your reading was better than my crappy one. I was insulted, to be honest. You make your own luck in life.'

'That's not always true,' Elizabeth replied.

Angela looked over at the *Dear Judith* book on the bedside table.

'And what are you reading? Eighties problems?'

'More like late-nineties ones,' she replied. 'Do you remember the whole *Dawson* craze?' she asked, touching her heart.

'Ugh, vile,' Angela replied. 'Is there anything juicy in there?'

'I haven't really gotten into it yet, but I get the feeling Judith was a no-nonsense kind of aunt.'

'Good, just what you need. Let me read it after you!'

'Now then, speaking of matters of the heart, how was...' she began to ask.

Paul poked his head around the door and Angela jumped.

'Sorry,' he said. 'Someone is here for Angela.'

'For me?' she asked with genuine surprise.

'In a red Jaguar convertible.'

'Oh,' Angela said.

She suddenly looked flustered.

'Don't you think you should go out there? Who is it?' Elizabeth asked.

'I suppose I better,' she said shuffling over to the door.

Elizabeth and Paul went to the small corridor window to take a look.

Outside, the car had its top down and the middle-aged man in the driving seat seemed to be relaxed and pleased with himself.

'What do you want, and how did you know I was living here?' Angela asked the man.

He said nothing but just looked her up and down and continued smiling to himself.

'Craig, I told you I'm not interested. If you think showing up here in a flashy car is suave, you're wrong, it's just creepy,' Angela said.

'How's flying?' he asked.

'How's being a sleazebag? You better get out of here, you're not impressing anyone,' she said becoming angrier.

She made sure he could see she was holding her iPhone.

'I'm not trying to impress anyone, but now that you mention it, want to come for a spin, Miss Eastfield?' he asked. 'It's a lot of fun.'

'No.'

'Suit yourself, I just thought I'd pay you a visit. We never had a chance to say goodbye, I just felt like it was unfinished business,' he said.

'Believe me, it's finished,' she said rolling her eyes.

'If that's what you want, I never could change your mind about anything once it was made up, could I? But that's what I always liked about you. Bye for now,' he said and pulled out of the driveway.

Back in the house, closing the door, Angela looked very annoyed.

'Who was that?' Elizabeth asked.

'My ex. Craig. He's a stockbroker and a complete scumbag. I can't believe he looked up my address,' she said.

'You broke up?' Elizabeth asked.

'As good as,' she replied.

'Are you okay? Come here,' she said and they hugged.

'Thanks, babe,' Angela said.

'Some people just can't put the past behind them,' she added, as much to herself as to Angela.

14

One of the lifts was different: it stopped on every floor. The sign said 'Shabbat Elevator'. The bar in the lobby was not especially busy, and Elizabeth recognised Trish immediately, as soon as she turned towards the reception, sitting next to Angela.

'Hiya, Elizabeth,' she gushed.

'Hey, Trish. Are you on the other crew then?'

'Yeah, we're leaving tomorrow morning. I think there's three crews over here actually. What do you think of this place then?'

Trish was stretched out next to a window as if she owned the place.

'It's a really nice hotel,' Elizabeth said.

'Not very crew-friendly, though. They put that shit on,' she said, pointing at the TV which was showing Israeli news. 'Have you been to the beach yet?' she asked.

'I'm planning on going tomorrow. I want to see Jerusalem today, didn't Angela tell you?'

'Is that far?' she asked.

'Not that far.'

'Oh, well, enjoy it. I'm just waiting for my supervisor to come down - the hotel lay on a shuttle bus for the beach.'

'See you later,' Elizabeth said, and walked over to the reception desk.

Bertie, a receptionist with short cropped hair, handed Elizabeth a map. He seemed to be a very friendly man who genuinely enjoyed helping people. Angela joined her, leaving Trish to her phone.

'What *is* the bitch talking about? Does she think she's still in Slough?' Angela said.

'Shh, I don't know! If the TV annoys her, she doesn't need to wait here. To be honest, I've had enough of hotels,' Elizabeth whispered.

Bertie wore an amused expression on his face.

'I know what you mean,' Angela said. 'They all start to seem the same after a while. Until I started flying, I'd stayed in three, max. But now it's every week, it's just another thing you do.'

'Mhm, it is a nice one though, a proper skyscraper.'

'Shall we get going?' Angela suggested.

'Yes, do we take the train over the road?'

'Yes, it's Tel Aviv HaShalom. Have a nice trip, ladies,' Bertie said.

Waving goodbye, they left through the glass revolving doors. The street was white-hot in the midday sun and the people outside moved slowly. Even the traffic lights seemed to work slowly, and it was as if the cars were melting into the road.

Angela and Elizabeth each drank a bottle of Highland Spring they had taken from the flight over, and outside the train station Angela lit a cigarette with a click function that changed its flavour to menthol.

'Dubai Duty Free,' she explained.

Suddenly Elizabeth started to worry that her outfit might appear a bit too revealing to look around religious sites. Indeed, the Old City in Jerusalem would turn out to be a different world altogether from Tel Aviv, but these different worlds were all strange to her in different ways. She felt as alien in a cosmopolitan, modern yet completely unfamiliar city like this as she would in Jerusalem.

The train journey took a long time and there were a lot of stops along the way. At Ramla, a large crowd of boys all wearing white shirts and black yarmulkes got off. Beyond the station, Elizabeth could see nothing but farmland and in the distance what seemed to be a village of white houses. A large woman in shorts and a blue t-shirt got on, took a seat opposite them. She was carrying a backpack and a small CD player playing upbeat eastern music out loud.

The old man sitting on the next row of seats turned and glared at her, folding up his newspaper. The woman gave him an indifferent stare, but turned the music down low anyway. Three young soldiers standing near the doors were chatting away, laughing, and as the train pulled away again, in spite of the noise, Angela started to nap resting her head on Elizabeth's shoulder. The first thing they did when they reached the train terminal in Jerusalem was stop for a burger. The heat seemed to have lessened.

'I need to get my strength up, there's a lot to see,' Angela said.

Elizabeth's phone beeped with a text message.

'Not Captain Timmy again?' Angela asked.

'Of course not, it's just from my mum,' she replied.

'I haven't met her yet, have I? I remember when your dad popped in, though.'

'She's a plastic surgeon, so my career choices have been a bit disappointing to say the least.'

'It could have been worse, and it's still early days. Do you think we'll both end up pushing a trolley at seventy?'

'Who knows. I'm not smart enough to do medicine. My brain can barely cope with first aid.'

'You did a degree, didn't you?' Angela asked.

'History,' she answered, nodding.

'Customer service jobs are the hardest jobs, whatever anyone says. You have to have a knack for it, it's not something you can just learn. Matt said he wants to be a photographer.'

Elizabeth took this as an indication that Angela was ready to talk about her date with him, a topic she had avoided until now.

'Good luck to him, then. With something like that, it's more who you know, though,' Elizabeth said.

'Probably. Can your mum do me a freebie, then? I need lipo,' Angela said with a serious expression on her face.

'Stop being insane, you don't need it at all. Besides, my mum only does skin work. She works in a burns unit in Euston.'

'Yeah, I need my skin fixed too, while we're at it. Botox or fillers or something, whatever it takes. You're lucky that your parents are still together.'

'Thirty years and still going strong.'

'It's lovely, I hope I can have that. Nobody seems happy with what they've got, or who they've got.'

'Don't start getting philosophical on me,' Elizabeth said.

'No, it's lovely.'

'Speaking of which, how *was* your afternoon with Matt? You haven't mentioned it much.'

'Well, like I said, he's a really nice guy... and cute in a way...'

'He is, but...?'

'Well I've thought about it and I just didn't feel that *spark*.'

'Oh well, you've still got Nicko's number! What's he like outside of work?'

'Matt?'

'Matt,' Elizabeth said.

'He's very friendly, very sweet...'

'But not your prince,' Elizabeth finished.

'Not my prince.'

'There *is* always Nicko,' Elizabeth suggested.

Angela did not reply.

They took a taxi to the Wailing Wall. The forecourt was crowded with visitors. In the streets nearby, groups of tourists and pilgrims as well as locals filled the narrow pavements. Elizabeth felt bloated from the fast food, and navigating around the crowds was overwhelming. She had remained in a pensive, brooding mood since the train journey, although she was not what she could call strictly 'unhappy'. This city, the centre of the spiritual world for millions of people, its very stones and somehow immediately familiar but distant scenery inspired a strange state of mind in her, optimism mixed with disappointment.

In the Church of the Holy Sepulchre, Elizabeth said a silent prayer in her head. Angela began to look bored and wore the same expression she had when Craig had shown up in his convertible: unimpressed and growing annoyed.

After a tour of the church, they took the tram to the modern part of the city. Angela splashed out on an expensive pair of sunglasses in a big department store.

'Am I sunburnt?' Angela asked.

Elizabeth realised that they must have spent about three hours outside.

'You're a bit pink,' she replied, looking at the back of her friend's neck.

'Better get some aftersun. I need some paracetamol, too, I feel a headache coming on.'

They stopped at Super-Pharm. Stepping back outside, Elizabeth looked down the road at the walls covered in graffiti. A warm breeze swept across the street, and the pair strolled on. A small market was winding down, and Elizabeth noticed an elderly woman in a hijab buying bread who seemed to be slightly stooped like a hunchback. It made her imagine herself when she would eventually become old. The woman noticed her staring and scowled so Elizabeth looked away.

They took a coach back to the Central Station in Tel Aviv and walked slowly back to the hotel.

* * *

On the flight back to London the passenger loads were low.

'Not a *bad* little trip, is it?' Angela asked when the first service was done.

'I really liked it there, there's a lot to see. And I like going anywhere for the first time, everything's exciting,' Elizabeth said.

'Yep, but the minibar last night was even more exciting. Mosques and churches are okay to a point... I think I went a bit overboard on the wine, though,' she said. 'Give me that,' she added pointing to one of the portable oxygen sets.

Elizabeth picked it up and Angela turned on the oxygen and inhaled deeply from the mask.

'Make sure nobody's coming,' she said peeking out of the closed curtain.

15

The crew room was almost empty, so it was very quiet when Elizabeth arrived at eight in the evening a few days later for her briefing for the night Moscow. After swiping in and printing off the latest notices, she left her bag next to the drop-boxes and looked for her name to check if there were any letters or notes. Inside her file-folder there was only one small white envelope that had her name written in block capitals on the front. She opened it and gasped.

Filth.

Disgusting home-wrecking whore.

Her face went white. She couldn't breathe. She could feel her chest tightening and turned and rushed out of the crew room still holding the note, leaving the drawer open. She sat in a toilet cubicle landside and looked at the note again. It was handwritten, but she did not recognise the writing. Was it a man's writing or a woman's? She decided to go straight home and phone in sick. Who was doing this, and why?

Elizabeth rushed back through the terminal to the Tube station. As her train left the station, her head was rushing with possibilities. An old man sat opposite her and smiled, but she could not return the smile. She was unable to concentrate. The words *disgusting* and *whore* ran through her head over and over again.

It had to be related to what had happened with Tim in Agadir. It had immediately and obviously occurred to her that Tim himself could have left the note, but it seemed extremely unlikely.

Wouldn't he be as 'guilty' of being promiscuous as her, and why risk leaving such an abusive letter even in a fit of anger? Could it have been a girlfriend of Tim's, another crew member? This seemed like a much more plausible possibility, but how would they know what had happened downroute?

Tim had promised to keep quiet about it, and there was nothing to be gained from talking about it. In any case he did not seem like the kind of person to take part in gossip. And why 'home-wrecking'? She was certain Tim was not married.

A fellow pilot? A jealous ex? She looked into her bag again at the note, taking care not to expose it to the view of the other passengers in the carriage. She looked carefully at the handwriting. It was impossible to say whether it had been a man or a woman, but the careful, planned shape of the letters meant that it had not been written quickly, there was no physical manifestation of anger there. This was a cold, calculated attack.

She exhaled slowly through her nose and closed her eyes. Her head felt painfully tight, and she took out the clips in her hair and let it down. She picked up her mobile when the train went above ground and called crewing.

'Hi, yes, I'm calling in sick for my duty, Moscow. Tonight. My staff number is 14737' she said.

The man sitting opposite was listening and smiled again, this time a knowing smile to himself, eyes down.

'Okay, Elizabeth, take care of yourself and just give us a call when you're feeling better to report fit for duty,' the woman in crewing said.

'Thank you,' she replied, and hung up.

As the train came to a stop at Hounslow West, she stood up and tossed her hair to one side. Her chest sunk and she moped off the train, making her way slowly to the stairs. When she got home she planned to go straight to bed with a cup of coffee to try to think everything through.

* * *

Dear Judith,

I'm 14 years old and I love playing the guitar. In fact, music is my whole life. I write my own music and lyrics.

I've been making a decent amount of money busking on the Underground and I know I want to do this for the rest of my life, but my parents insist I stay on at school and get my exams.

How can I explain that music is what I want to do with my life? School is meaningless to me.

Chris, Islington

Elizabeth skimmed the reply. Predictably, Judith's advice was for Chris to finish his studies so that he would have something to fall back on, and then try to pursue a career in the music industry when he was older.

At some point, Elizabeth had stopped bothering to read the advice, and now just read the problems. She felt jealous of Chris from Islington in a strange way - he had a passion and he knew exactly what it was, and to go with it he had the confidence to get out there and do what he loved in front of the public. At fourteen he had already known what it was he wanted to do with the rest of his life. Almost ten years older than that, Elizabeth still felt like she had no idea.

She looked again at the picture of the smiling agony aunt on the back of the book. What a strange, but all the same *fitting* souvenir of Agadir. In her top drawer lay that other souvenir, like a piece of evidence from a crime scene, the note. She had decided to keep it until she got to the bottom of the situation however much she wanted to just set fire to it on the garden barbecue and forget it had ever existed, but moving on seemed out of reach.

Whoever had written it and left it in her drop-box had got exactly what they must have intended. Elizabeth felt utterly demoralised.

Someone out there knew what she had done, and wanted her to know that they disapproved of the transgression in the strongest terms. She decided to take the rest of the week off, and when she felt better, she would get back to work and get on with studying for the recurrent. She just felt like being alone, and now being off work sick brought an palpable if small measure of relief. She took a Nytol pill from the packet and drank it with her coffee.

She wondered what Chris from Islington was doing now. So few people end up making it in the entertainment industry. Maybe he was something sensible like an accountant or a lawyer and thought back to his days as a teenage busker - playing for the donations of admiring commuters on the Tube - only from time to time. Probably when his mind wandered off the e-mails and spreadsheets.

Or maybe he had made it.

What is success, anyway? she wondered, mouthing the word 'success' slowly several times before drifting off to sleep.

16

'There she is!' Bob shouted from behind the desk.

Elizabeth came down the concrete stairs into the basement gym taking care not to slip in her newish pink Nikes. It was busy that evening: the music was already pumping from a dock, and people were warming up around the room; some skipping, others stretching, and there were a few just standing around chatting and gesturing, trying to make themselves heard above the blare of David Guetta.

'That'll be ten pounds please, miss!' Bob said.

Elizabeth handed him the note and placed her backpack on the floor next to the bench.

'How's everything?' he asked.

'Yeah, good, and you?' she replied.

'I'm on top of the world! Been up to much? You haven't been in for ages.'

'I've just been so busy with work, and moving out near the airport means it takes me a lot longer to come into town.'

'It's okay, just pop in whenever you need a class,' Bob said.

He was joined at the desk by Thomas, the other trainer and manager of the gym.

'Hi, Thomas,' she said.

'Elizabeth, you're alive! Great to see you,' he said, and

patted her on the back.

'Right let's get this started. Everybody find a space and let's warm up,' said Bob as he clapped his hands together loudly.

Elizabeth threw herself into the warm up and broke out in a sweat. She had been exercising irregularly, but only now realised how far she had let her fitness slip while flying. It was necessarily erratic: she had odd days off, and irregular hours spent flying. She made up her mind to fix a regular time to exercise on her days off, to mark them on her roster and get back into the habit. Aside from the obvious physical benefits, she missed the vibe of the class, and she missed seeing Bob and Thomas. Both of them had been so kind and motivated her to shift the weight she had put on in her final year of university. She thought back to the first day she had been to the kickboxing club. It was a Wednesday night and she had been meaning to attend for a long time after first seeing the gym online. After a few visits, it had become like a second home to her.

Elizabeth looked around. It seemed like an eternity had passed since those first sessions because everything looked different. The gym was redecorated and full of new faces, but the format of the classes had thankfully stayed the same. When it was time for pair work, she teamed up with a Swedish woman called Klara who had been a regular since long before Elizabeth started.

'How's it going, Klara?' she asked, putting on her gloves after taking a sip of water.

'Very fine, very fine. It's nice to see you at kickboxing after so long. Are you still in your air hostess job?'

'Yeah, I don't know for how long, though,' she said.

'I see. You're not enjoying it? Klara asked.

'I'm just not sure if it's... a job for life.'

'Is she moaning already?' Bob said, overhearing the conversation and skipping over. 'Look, Liz, don't come in here with your negativity,' he teased.

'This is girl talk, butt out!' said Klara.

'It's not like I have much to complain about,' she lied. 'But let's just say the novelty factor wears off quickly.'

'You'll be fine, straight shots, everyone! With power!' Bob yelled.

In time with the music, Elizabeth punched Klara's pads with as much force as she could muster. After several shots, the muscles in her upper arms started to ache sharply and she felt the burning in her abdomen that she recalled from previous sessions.

'Go with it, through the pain! Give it all you've got! Attack!' Bob shrieked.

Elizabeth reached deep inside herself, summoning the stamina and continued to dish out explosive shots into the pads in time with the Michael Jackson song that was now coming from the dock.

'That's it. Let it out, girl,' Klara said.

The electronic bell sounded.

'Okay, time. Move around, use this as your rest. The ones with pads get your gloves on and vice versa,' Bob said.

Elizabeth was panting.

'You exhausted me!' said Klara. She started to shake off her arms. 'You must have a lot of anger stored up.'

'I must have.'

A tall, fairly skinny man walked over.

'You really went for it!' said the man.

'Cheers,' she replied.

'She's making up for all the classes she's missed,' Bob muttered.

'I'm Chip,' he said.

'Elizabeth,' she replied with a nod.

The electronic bell sounded again. It was Elizabeth's turn to hold the pads for Klara to hit.

Towards the end of the session, when warming down, after ab work, Chip caught Elizabeth's eye and flashed her a wide, sincere grin. She found herself unable to resist smiling back. Meeting guys in the kickboxing gym was not an idea she had ever really entertained. There were several huge disadvantages, not least the fact that she was wearing minimal makeup, and normally covered in sweat from the warm up onwards. It was mostly that it seemed to attract the kind of men who were - albeit to differing extents - obsessed with fighting. Something about that ruled them out as simply not a 'type' Elizabeth would normally think of dating.

Chip came over with a towel on his shoulders. His hair was dark and stringy with sweat which also darkened his striped t-shirt.

'Well, I'm absolutely finished!' he said.

'Tell me about it, it's been months since I've had a workout that intense,' Elizabeth replied.

'So what do you do?'

'She's a trolley-dolly, stay away!' Bob called out, and Elizabeth faked a dismissive pout in response.

'It's true, I'm cabin crew,' she sighed.

'It's a small world, I'm in air traffic control at Heathrow,' he said.

'Seriously?' she asked, wondering if he was making some kind of joke.

'Yes, seriously I am. It's a boring job, but...' he didn't have time to finish.

'Who said you could come into my class and chat up my female members?' Bob said putting his arm around Chip. They both laughed.

'I'm just being sociable,' he said.

'It really is summertime,' Bob mused, and went back to saying his goodbyes to the attendees who were leaving.

'Well, nice to meet you,' said Chip.

'Yeah, see you next week,' Elizabeth replied as she put her backpack on one shoulder and dropped the empty water bottle in the bin, her mind and body refreshed by the exercise. She tried not to think about getting home and dealing with having to think about the note that was still in her top drawer, but now she could see things more logically: it had happened, it was real.

Just be patient. Wait and see what's next and deal with it when it comes - that's how to handle this, she thought, and tried to believe it was possible.

17

It was during that week off that Elizabeth began to feel as though her surroundings, the house itself, were somehow going crazy, as if there was something in the air which was an external reflection of her inner state, akin to living in a madhouse.

She texted Tim to invite him over in order to see if he could shed any light on the note. She needed information. She needed resolution. It was certain that he would be willing to meet up in person.

Angela had been shacked up in her room, the largest in the house, with Nicko since the night before. Elizabeth could hear the sounds of a football match with Dutch commentary through the wall, and every so often he would cheer or groan, reacting loudly.

Elizabeth imagined the effect on Angela, who hated all sport. She left her room to go downstairs to check if she had any post when she was startled by a rumble and then a high-pitched scream from above.

'Well you need to LEARN IT SOMEWHERE!' Angela shrieked as her bedroom door burst open.

Nicko sped down the stairs with his leather overnight bag in his hand and marched out of the house, slamming the door behind him. It was so loud that the windows shook. Elizabeth barely had time to register who had just raced past her. She looked up the stairs at the sight of Angela, mascara streaming down her face, her eyes wet with tears. She looked devastated.

'What happened? Are you okay?' she asked in

astonishment.

'No. I slapped him. I...' she trailed off into sobs.

Elizabeth walked up the stairs and put her arm around her friend. Angela had become invisible in the house whenever she was hosting Nicko, but the situation was understandable. She was in a distance relationship and she would not be able to see him at all for long stretches of time.

'Why did you slap him? What did he do?' Elizabeth asked.

'He...' Angela could not finish. She just nestled into Elizabeth's embrace and sobbed, long and hard.

'Is everything okay? I heard a bang?' It was Paul, who had emerged from his room downstairs.

'I don't know,' replied Elizabeth.

'I'm sorry, I'm sorry,' Angela muttered. 'He didn't deserve it, but I just lost my temper. And now he's gone,' she added.

'I'm sure it's nothing, just a small misunderstanding,' Elizabeth offered.

'You didn't see his eyes afterwards. He looked like he wanted to kill me.'

Elizabeth had no idea what to say. What had he done to make her slap him?

'Maybe it's because you've both been cooped up together for so long,' she said.

'Maybe. You're probably right. I need a drink.'

'Do you want some water?' asked Paul.

'Wine,' she croaked.

They walked slowly downstairs, and Elizabeth took an unopened bottle of white wine out of the fridge. Angela took two glasses from the cupboard.

'Wine?' Elizabeth asked Paul.

'No thanks, I'm a little bit busy. Are you sure you are good?' he asked.

'No, but I will be,' she replied, taking a shiny packet of menthol Vogues from their carton and a gold lighter from her shelf in the cupboard, quickly slipping off the plastic wrapping.

They went into the garden. The sun was setting and the sky was mauve. They sat on the plastic garden chairs.

'It's beautiful at this time of day,' Elizabeth said, pouring two glasses of wine out on the slab of concrete that covered the drain - it had long served as a defacto small table. A red Emirates 380 glided overhead.

Angela let out a large, thick cloud of smoke and looked up at the plane dramatically.

'Do you know what I've realised?' she asked. 'The problem is me. I'm the one...' she stopped to take another deep drag. 'I do this in every relationship. I try to be the boss. No compromises. No wonder they...'

She started to sob again into her wine.

'I'm sure you'll patch things up, don't worry,' Elizabeth said, although it did not sound as convincing as she wanted it to.

She thought about the way Angela and Nicko had met, in that very garden. It had only been a short time, but the intensity of their bond was striking - it was passionate, and now it had literally become violent. In that time, Angela had all but ditched Elizabeth.

'I'm sorry I've been spending all my time with Nicko, that's not on,' she said as if she had been reading her mind.

'He's your boyfriend. Some things are special,' she said.

'No, it's just not on. I wouldn't expect the same from you. Could you see if he's texted me, please?' she asked handing Elizabeth her mobile. 'I can't look.'

'No new messages.'

'Try WhatsApp, babe.'

'Still nothing,' Elizabeth said.

Angela stuck her chin out and inhaled through her nostrils holding the cigarette vertically.

'I must look a total mess,' she gasped.

'Yep!' Elizabeth said, and they both laughed.

Angela's phone started to ring. She answered. She didn't say a word. She hung up.

'What happened?' Elizabeth asked.

'It's over,' Angela said expressionless, and burst into a fresh flood of tears.

There was a knock at the front door and Elizabeth went to answer it. Tim stood there.

'I texted you because I needed to ask you about something,' Elizabeth said.

'I was worried something like this would happen,' he said.

'Come upstairs to my room,' Elizabeth said, closing the door behind him.

* * *

'So your wife is ill. So you pretend you don't have a wife,' she said.

'She knows: I have her permission,' was his succinct reply.

Elizabeth's head was racing.

'She always knew she had her condition, scoliosis, and when we got married we'd already agreed that when this time came...' he started.

Elizabeth found it strange that there was no sense of sadness in his eyes. He was so matter-of-fact.

'When she became unable to be physically independent...'

'You don't love her,' she said.

'Of course I love my wife. She's the only woman I've ever loved. Of course I don't talk about what I've done after the fact, I know it might risk upsetting her, so I keep quiet about it.'

Elizabeth bit her bottom lip.

'Just because I sleep with someone doesn't mean I feel anything for them, they're two different things.'

Elizabeth took the note out of her drawer and handed it to him. Tim looked it over and frowned.

'I was worried Agnes might do something like this.'

'Your wife?'

'No,' he said. 'Agnes is a friend of my wife's who works on reception in the crew centre. She confronted me directly and there was no telling her anything, she was furious.'

'And how did she know to go after me?' Elizabeth asked. 'You must have told her...' she began.

'No, she already knew. Someone must have been gossiping.'

The only person Elizabeth had told was the person sitting outside crying and chainsmoking, and it couldn't have been her, it was simply not possible. But then again, could she have let something slip inadvertently?

'Did you tell anyone, Tim?' Elizabeth asked him as seriously as she could.

'I don't talk about that stuff to anyone,' he replied.

'Honestly?'

'I never would,' he said handing the note back to Elizabeth. 'Either someone saw something and speculated, or you let it slip. I'll speak to Agnes and there won't be any more notes, you can rest assured,' he stated.

'How do you know?' she asked.

'Unless she wants to start looking for a new job...'

'Oh, I see. Tim, thanks for being frank with me. I'm not judging you,' she said.

'Yes you are, that's what people do. People judge, whether they like it or not. That's people.'

'I was just so shaken up, it was all so sinister. I think I'm still in a bit of shock, it's silly... But thank you for clearing everything up,' she said.

'Speaking of which, have you had your check-ups done recently?' he asked.

'What?!'

'I'm joking, just a joke!' he smiled.

She punched him lightly on the shoulder.

'But seriously, you should not have had to deal with all that. If you get any more notes or if she says anything to you...'

'I'll let you know,' Elizabeth said.

'Make sure you do,' he said and gave her a peck on the cheek.

The excitement Elizabeth had felt on the trip was completely absent. She felt nothing except for relief, and more than a little sorry for Tim's wife. Later in the evening, over more wine, Angela denied saying anything about what had happened to anyone, swore to it, but Elizabeth could not shake the feeling that it was not the entire truth.

18

After entering her hotel room in Beirut and locking the door behind her, Elizabeth pulled up a seat next to the window to watch the rain falling lightly outside on the mountaintops and to have a quiet moment to herself before unpacking and changing out of her uniform. Ten minutes later, another member of her crew, Christine, knocked on the door. She was smiling nervously.

'Hiya, Liz, I was just wondering if you could help me?'

'Christine, what's wrong?'

'It's nothing, I just wanted a favour,' she muttered.

'Sure, what can I do?'

'I just saw on Facebook that the Christmas and New Year's rosters are out. Oh my God, oh my God!' she said with her hand on top of her doughnut hairstyle.

'They're out this far in advance? That's very early, I didn't know they scheduled it so early. You look a bit... Is everything okay?' Elizabeth asked.

'I don't want to be abroad on Christmas Day, I need to be with my family,' she replied, her eyes full of tears. 'I can't. I can't.'

'That's why you're upset. What did they give you? Four sectors?'

'I don't know yet, I haven't checked it. I can't.'

'What do you mean, you can't?' Elizabeth asked.

'Can you check it *for* me?' she asked suddenly looking Elizabeth straight in the eyes and putting her hand on her shoulder. 'Pleeease?'

'Yeah, of course I can, but do you want me to tell you if it's good news or bad news? What do you want me to do?'

'I don't know, I don't know!' she squealed, jumping up and down.

'Don't panic, I can read it for you.'

'Oh my God, thank you, babe. I feel like I'm going out of my mind.' She started shaking her head. She looked traumatised.

They walked next door to Christine's room. Although the design was identical to her own room, something about it immediately struck Elizabeth as somehow off. As she glanced around she noticed that there were tartan throws everywhere. Where there had been leaflets and Beirut tourism magazines, in their place were packets of Walker's crisps and Cadbury's chocolate bars. Next to the TV was a giant pink teddybear with a heart on its stomach which seemed slightly sinister to Elizabeth. She looked over at the wall that the bed was lined up against. It had been adorned with a cutesy One Direction poster.

'What have you done with the room?' she asked in astonishment.

'I get homesick if I don't make my hotel room as much like home as I can. On five-day trips like this one in the middle of nowhere it gets really...' and she pulled a pained face. She sat on the side of the bed and handed her laptop to Elizabeth.

'I've logged in. Go on, get it up, I can't do it! I can't look!'

Elizabeth clicked on the display icon and saw at once that Christine had won the jackpot in terms of rostering. She had no duties on Christmas Day, plus a week off over New Year. She looked over at her anguished face.

'Hun, don't tell me. I want *just you* to know for a while,' Christine explained going into a nasal voice.

A long silence followed.

'This is ridiculous, why don't you just...'

'No, I can't know! Don't say anything, it's too much,' she said, and the tears started again. 'My mum needs me at home!'

'Is she ill?' Elizabeth asked.

'No,' sobbed Christine.

After a long, stunned silence, Elizabeth went over to the bathroom to get her some tissues from the dispenser.

'I'm sorry, it's just so... I mean I just can't...' She could not go on.

Elizabeth sat down on the bed next to her and closed the laptop. She decided to just tell her the good news and put her out of her misery.

'You're off on the 25th and you have a week off over New Year,' she said in a neutral tone, and waited for it to sink in.

The sobs got louder and louder, Christine pushed her head onto Elizabeth's shoulder.

'I said you're off! Don't cry, it's good news. You couldn't have done better than that, everyone will be offering you cash to swap with them.'

'I know, I'm just so happy,' she said, her body shaking.

* * *

Elizabeth had gone back to her room and unpacked slowly. How quickly it had become a routine and something she did automatically, packing and unpacking, with no thought at all involved. She made a cup of peppermint tea and looked outside again.

After two rings, Elizabeth picked up the phone.

'Hiya, babe, it's me, do you still want to go to the shopping centre?' Christine asked.

'Yeah, how long will it take you to get ready? I need about fifteen, twenty minutes I'd say,' Elizabeth said.

'Same. I've got some new fake eyelashes I wanna try out. I'll give you a knock when I'm done, babe. City Mall here we come! Whoop!'

Elizabeth went into the bathroom and looked at her face in the mirror. She looked pale and tired, there was no getting around the fact. She was not in the mood to socialise. She was the opposite of whoop.

She leaned right in towards her reflection and looked at the bags under her eyes, taking in the damage. There was a world of difference between her face now and her face as it had been only a few months before: the chapped, cracked lips an unsightly and obvious symptom of dehydration, her cheeks' elasticity reducing gradually.

What a depressing, depressing sight, she thought.

She picked up the expensive cream with hyaluronic acid her mother had given her from on top of her plastic 100ml bag and squeezed a large splodge onto the back of her hand. She massaged the cream into her whole face and her neck with rough sweeps and sat on the edge of the bath next to the glass shower screen gazing into the hallway as it burned into her skin.

The size of the hotel rooms was more than generous, they even had small kitchen areas sectioned off with a cooker, a microwave, a fridge and freezer. Elizabeth felt small and weak in such an expanse. She felt defeated.

She thought of Christine in the next room who would be getting ready, getting excited about going to the mall in one of her best outfits, giving the eyelashes their trial run. Elizabeth had never felt so alone.

When they got into the cab outside the hotel reception, the rain had started to fall rather heavily, and the mountains surrounding the hotel looked greyed and peaceful. The driver could only speak a few words of English, to Christine's dismay. Apparently she was now in a chatty mood.

'It's so pretty with all the rain and hills and trees and everything' she said. The driver did not react.

The roads were not as busy as Elizabeth remembered from a previous stay, and when they arrived outside the mall, Elizabeth wondered if it was a public holiday and whether or not it would actually be open. Inside, they wandered around taking in their surroundings, and stopped for a coffee in Second Cup where the atmosphere was quiet and the air conditioning was particularly strong.

Christine looked down at her cappuccino and took out her cigarettes.

'Smoking allowed!' she exclaimed. 'You can't do that in Prêt à Ming-er.'

Is she joking? Elizabeth thought. *Maybe she's not.*

'It's a smoking culture,' Christine said, seeming to quote someone.

'Are you going to get anything or shall we just do window shopping?' Elizabeth asked.

'Well we deffo need to take a look at the make up counters, 'cause the girls over here totes know what they're doing when it comes to cosmetics, don't they?'

Elizabeth nodded. 'It's been a long time since I've seen one of those,' she said pointing at the Virgin Megastore opposite the café.

Christine shrugged.

'We can have a look if you want, I need to see if I can get some bits and bobs to take back home. The prices are decent over here,' she said.

'Let's ask Mike and Josh if we can get some time in the Duty Free before we fly back, I might get some wine and chocolates, or Castania nuts,' Elizabeth said.

'Good idea, but we need at least fifteen minutes otherwise it's like *Supermarket Sweep* and I hate that. You know, for an older guy, Mike's quite fit.'

Elizabeth could not tell whether Christine was making fun of her over what had happened with Tim and the fallout. If anyone actually did know what had happened, and it was perfectly possible, if they talked about it then it was probably still a fresh topic for gossip. There was no way Elizabeth could know what people said about her behind her back so she had decided to not worry about it. Christine was probably innocent, so she gave her the benefit of the doubt.

'Josh is young but he's not a fitty,' Christine added.

'He's okay. Do you have a boyfriend?'

'Well I've got my Dwayne, but the night is still young as they say. We're still just dating, really. He does stay over sometimes, though,' she added with a wink.

'Don't you live with your parents?'

'Yeah, but it's alright: they're crew,' she explained, the volume of her voice rising. 'It's so embarrassing, but when we first started seeing each other we used to Skype every night, you know, hours every night. And one time,' she started giggling, 'I fell asleep with Skype still running!'

'Do you snore?'

'Nooo, but it's so embarrassing,' Christine squeaked, stomping her feet under the table in hysterics. Some of the other customers looked around and Elizabeth finally lightened up and laughed.

'He's a babe, my Dwayne - a car mechanic - but set me up with one of these captains or first class passengers, and I'd be off like a shot!'

She paused and looked thoughtful.

'It's a bit bad, innit?'

'It's your life,' Elizabeth said. She had never had to worry about money, and who was she to judge what other women found attractive? Christine was only about twenty, and it occurred to Elizabeth that someone so young shouldn't feel in a rush to settle down. Elizabeth's own situation, on the other hand, felt more pressing, and every day she was preoccupied by it more and more. She considered putting a bit more effort into dating seriously. *Ageing sneaks up on people and catches them off guard*, she reflected.

A man and a woman came into the café speaking loud English. Christine perked up again.

'Look it's Josh and Philippa! Hey guys!'

Elizabeth turned. The first officer, Josh, and the purser, Philippa, who were both about ten years older than Elizabeth turned at the same time and noticed that they were not alone.

'Ladies, this is a coincidence,' Josh said.

'I didn't hear from you, you should have left a note under my door if you were going to go out,' Philippa said.

'It's okay, I think Beirut is pretty safe, whatever people say,' Elizabeth said.

'No worries, I want a nice, calm little trip. Are you doing your early Christmas shopping? I saw the rosters were out -

seems so far off, but really it's not. This place is very chic,' she said.

'Well, we weren't planning on doing a big shop,' Christine lisped in a mock-camp voice. 'Just make up and gossip! I hope you guys don't mind all my smoke.'

'Not at all. I'm in the Christmas spirit,' Josh said lifting up his plastic bags.

'What did you ge-e-et?!' Christine asked, looking more and more excited.

'Ha, they're not Christmas presents, it's just some little things for my kids. I found some pop-up books for them, they're twins, fourth birthday coming up, and a nice scarf for my wife so she doesn't feel left out,' he said.

'And a Justin Bieber CD for me!' Philippa added. 'Let's get a table for four, you don't mind if we join you, do you?'

'Of course not,' Christine said lighting up her second Marlboro Light.

They talked and looked at some make up. Josh seemed very bored but he was trying not to show it. Elizabeth spent some time before going back to the hotel messaging with Angela who informed her that Matt had specifically asked for Elizabeth's number to ask her on a date. She wondered if that had possibly upset Angela, but Angela reassured her that it was fine. As quickly as they had fought, she and Nicko had made up.

19

'Visitor for you,' Paul called up the stairs to Elizabeth.

Matt was wearing a white shirt, a black skinny tie and on his face was a warm smile.

'Hey,' he said.

'Matt, you look very smart. You're a bit early,' Elizabeth said, feeling completely underdressed. 'You have to let me just change and then I'm ready to go. Do you want to wait with Paul?' she asked.

'Come to the kitchen. I'm cooking, you can help me,' Paul said, taking the hint.

Elizabeth bounced back up the stairs and rummaged through the dresses on her clothes rack. Everything was going wrong. She could hear Paul making small talk with Matt downstairs, Matt's deep voice reverberating up the stairs.

Why is he dressed like that, she thought, *we're just going to the high street... and this is Hounslow, not Park Lane. Why am I freaking out, anyway? This was just supposed to be a casual date. There's no time to think, get changed, it already looks crazy.*

She could hear that Angela and Nicko's conversation had stopped in the next room. Had she told him that she went on a date with Matt after she had already met him in the garden for the first time? Doubtful. Was it an uncomfortable silence?

Elizabeth continued to rummage through the outfits on the rack and finally decided on an understated blue dress that went well with her black jacket and put on her small amethyst pendant. She was starting to perspire a little and tried to breathe out the annoyance and cool down. She spritzed on some Coco Noir, grabbed her phone and handbag and closed the bedroom door slowly to avoid slamming it.

'He's always making us delicious things,' Elizabeth said looking at the cookie dough Matt was stirring. 'Paul is the ideal housemate, it's just that it's no good for our figures,' she added through the kitchen door.

'Not true. I just bake when I have some free time,' Paul said holding the wooden spoon aloft with a look of pride on his face that was obvious.

'Elizabeth, you look amazing,' Matt said. Elizabeth detected a little embarrassment which made her feel embarrassed in turn.

'Where are we going, then? Do you feel in the mood for pizza?' she asked.

'I'm not too fussy,' he replied.

'There's a South Indian restaurant over the road, if you like?' she suggested.

'Have you been there before?' Matt asked.

'Nope, just passed by.'

'That one, I've heard it's very good,' Paul said.

'Sounds good, let's go there,' Matt said.

'Settled. See you later, Paul,' Elizabeth said as they walked to the door.

The restaurant was very close to the house, less than five minutes on foot, and the place was not busy.

'No Angela at home, then?' he asked when they had taken their seats.

'She's in, but Nicko's over, so she's locked away as usual,' Elizabeth explained.

'Cosy,' Matt said.

'I'm surprised they don't get cabin fever. When he's over here, you don't see either of them, they're in their cocoon.'

It occurred to her, thinking back to Angela's slap outburst, that this wasn't exactly true, but she didn't want to gossip.

'It's romantic, though, I'm glad she's happy,' he said.

'I suppose. It all happened very suddenly,' she said trying to think of something to change the subject to.

'Do you think something that starts quickly can last?' he asked.

'What burns bright burns fast - isn't that what they say? Anyway, what would I know?' Elizabeth said.

'When I went out in town with Angela, I didn't feel any... chemistry, and I can't say I'm let down. I was flattered to be asked though. I hope it works out for her,' he said.

Elizabeth could see that he meant it, but now she was aware that Matt would be wondering if there was any chemistry with *her*. Did anyone honestly enjoy dates? They always felt like a test. Did that mean that she wanted there to be chemistry?

'This menu looks amazing. My mouth is literally watering,' he said.

'I've been living here for over a year, so it's sort of amazing I didn't try it sooner. That's the thing about always being away. I love Indian food,' she said with a smile of approval.

'Can I get you any drinks?' the waiter asked. He was wearing a long white jacket and had a regal air. He lit the candle on the table with a tiny Bic lighter. It lit first time.

'Just a sparkling water,' Elizabeth started.

'Same for me, please,' asked Matt. 'Could we take the mixed starters?' he added.

'Certainly,' the waiter said, and then returned to the kitchen and dimmed the lights in the restaurant slightly.

Matt's brown eyes flickered in the candlelight, and the ambiance of the lighting made him look slightly younger. He was certainly endearing. To Elizabeth he now seemed cute: she could understand what had caught Angela's attention when Matt had passed them in the crewroom at Heathrow.

'Please don't tell me you're on a diet,' he said. 'Tonight I want a feast!' he said.

'Special occasion?'

'Funny. I am starving though!'

'Did you have any flights today?' Elizabeth asked.

'I had home standby and got stood down two hours in - I guess they realised I'd be out of hours if they gave me anything.

Clear all day. I have a three day Copenhagen coming up, so I was worried I'd lose it.'

'Copenhagen is a lovely city,' she said.

'Lovely but expensive,' Matt said. 'The allowances aren't bad, though. The hotel's nice, too. Good photo opportunities.'

'My non-flying friends can't believe we get paid for doing nothing,' she said.

'Were they pleased for you when you told them you got the job?'

'Yeah, it was like a dream come true. It wasn't my *childhood* dream to be an air hostess, but it ticks a lot of boxes.'

'I'll be completely honest with you,' he said, 'I'm not planning on sticking around in the job much longer.' On his face he wore a slight expression of worry.

The waiter came back with a shiny metal serving container crammed with dips and snacks, and a separate stack of freshly made popadams.

'Thank you,' they both said simultaneously.

'Tuck in!' Matt said.

'Delicious,' Elizabeth said nibbling on a spiral-shaped murukku. 'So where are you going? What are you going to do?'

'I've just had enough,' he said. 'Nothing dramatic, but I don't see any prospect of promotion, and I don't like being away all the time any more. Don't get me wrong, I love my trips, but there's no consistency. I can't remember what a weekend feels like because I'm forced to never have them.' He paused. 'Sorry to spend the dinner moaning,' he said.

'No problem, it's the same thing I've noticed anyway. Do you have another job lined up?' she asked.

'Nope, and *that's* a problem!' he laughed.

'So,' Elizabeth said, glancing over at a photo on the wall, a panoramic shot of the rivers in Kerala, 'Angela told me your passion is photography.'

'Yep, that's true,' Matt said as he played with a piece of popadam. 'But trying to do that as a full time career, freelance, would be taking a huge risk,' he said.

They finished off the starters and Elizabeth took a long sip of sparkling water.

'So that's me,' he said. 'You're still enjoying it, aren't you?' he asked.

'Sure, no complaints from me.'

'Any favourite destinations?' he asked.

'That's a tough call. I love Tehran,' she said, and Matt squinted at her with a confused look on his face.

'You must be the only one who does, right?'

'I could be. It's just so peaceful and seems so much like home... just *not*,' she attempted to explain.

'I know what you mean,' he said. 'Don't you mind wearing a headscarf?' he asked.

'No, not at all. I think it's quite glamorous.'

'I suppose it depends how you wear it.'

'I'm not a big drinker, either, so that side doesn't bother me,' she said.

'Me neither. Crew love to complain, *I'm cold, I'm bo-o-ored, I'm sick of these people...* but you just have to take the rough with the smooth,' he said. 'This job is a magnet for divas.'

'What is it the trainers said every five minutes? It's swings and roundabouts,' she said.

Matt laughed in recognition. 'They were right, it is swings and roundabouts, but that's to be expected. That's like anything else in life, flying isn't an exception, it just makes certain things more intense when you're in the air. I think a lot of the crew have never had any other job, that might have a lot to do with it.'

'What main course did you want?' she asked.

'I was too busy chatting to have a proper look. I like the look of the masala dosa,' he said.

'Coconut paneer for me,' she said. 'Coconut is supposed to be a superfood.'

'Paneer is cheese, isn't it?'

'Yes. It's great stuff.'

The waiter took their orders, and removed the used plates and containers from the table leaving only the metal pot of unfinished mango chutney behind.

'I'll say one thing, this place is a hidden gem...' Matt started.

'Hidden next to a rough road on the outskirts of the

airport, I know. I only decided to live here so I have to spend as little of my life commuting as possible. Getting around the airport is enough in itself,' she said.

'Heathrow is the gateway to Hell!' Matt said.

A family came in and sat down near the windows.

'Have you thought about taking a period of extended leave to go over your options?' she asked. 'Something like a sabbatical?'

'I could ask, it's one possibility, or I could go part time and try to find something else in addition to flying,' he said. 'Keep my foot in the door, so to speak.'

'Hm.' Elizabeth had only known of one other person to leave during her time at the airline, and that person had been asked to do a secondment and just never returned. Suddenly she felt some pressure on her foot, and she realised that it was Matt.

He shuffled and pulled his leg back quickly.

'Oh, I'm so sorry,' he said.

'It's okay!' she said.

'No, I didn't mean to,' he said.

'I know, it's okay!'

An awkward silence followed.

'Do you feel like you'd be losing your social life if you left the airline?' she asked, trying to move on quickly.

'No, I don't have tonnes of friends, and most of them are

people I knew before I started flying.'

'I see,' Elizabeth said. She looked at Matt and took his face in.

Angela was right, Matt was handsome. He had a lean face, and large eyes that gave him a certain intelligence. He had the subtlest hint of stubble which balanced his look with a touch of masculinity. His eyebrows were his best feature - they gave him attractive, curious expressions, and when he was relaxed, their arches rounded out the angularity of his face. The overall effect was charming. He noticed her looking, so she looked down at the tablecloth.

'No Sandra at home today?' he asked.

'Do you like her?' Elizabeth asked, regretting her sarcasm as soon as the question left her lips.

'She's not my type at all, but she's famous in the airline. There's nobody quite like Sandra!' he said.

Elizabeth nodded.

'Underneath all the melodrama and *Showgirls* nails, she's a kind-hearted person, believe me,' she said. 'She's staying with her mum in Berlin at the moment.'

'What's it like living with her?' he asked.

'So many people ask me that when they find out we're housemates! She's a sweetheart. She takes flying very seriously. I know it was *her* childhood dream. And she's been through a lot in life.'

'Aw, good for her,' he said.

The main courses arrived. The dosa Matt had ordered was huge and went far beyond the edges of the serving plate. It came with a creamy coconut chutney dotted with black mustard seeds and a spicy, watery soup in a larger metal bowl.

'That must be the sambar, I suppose it's to dip it in. Tuck in, this looks amazing,' he said.

'It's gorgeous,' she said, looking him directly in the eyes.

The conversation turned from colleagues to family. When Elizabeth told Matt that her mother was a surgeon, he nodded his head in a knowing gesture.

'You're from a smart family, then.'

'I guess you could say that,' she replied.

'I knew you were intelligent, you can see it in the eyes,' he explained.

'Is that a scientific fact? You wouldn't want to see my face when I first wake up, before my make up goes on,' she said.

A silence.

'What I mean is, it takes a lot of work to bring out a girl's features,' she explained.

'Fair enough. Although some of the male crew have been known to employ tinted moisturiser,' he said. 'No comment.'

She snickered.

'It's what's inside that counts. It's the oldest cliché in the book, but I really believe that, and try to live by it,' she added.

'I second that,' he said.

'This stuff is delicious, I need to finally get around to learning how to cook, I've been meaning to for years,' she said.

'Well you can ask Paul to teach you. You wouldn't have any problem sourcing the ingredients, living here.'

'Yeah, Paul's the cook, really. I don't want to cramp his style. Sandra sometimes used to make German stuff like schnitzels. My culinary skills go about as far as ordering on Just Eat.'

'The wonders of technology. Do you have the app?'

Elizabeth laughed.

'It doesn't go that far. I've been trying not to live on my phone. The way loads of people have become smartphone zombies scares me. We're becoming too dependent.'

'Maybe. I know I couldn't live without my phone. To be honest, I can't remember the time before we all had them.'

'I had a personal trainer, briefly, when I lived at home. He was this huge, Hungarian guy,' Elizabeth said.

'Oh yeah?'

'Anyway, his girlfriend was the jealous type.'

Matt nodded.

'So, she used the GPS on his phone to stalk him, basically, if 'stalk' is the right word. She tracked his whereabouts and called him all the time asking why he was spending so much time *here*, and what was he doing *there*...'

'And they broke up?'

'It was inevitable. I'm not blaming the technology, but it does bring out the dark side in some people.'

'I don't have a dark side,' he said.

'We all do, Matt, you just haven't revealed yours yet.'

'No, not at this stage, at least!'

'Hey, have some more of the rice, please. I can't eat all this,' she said spooning heaps of bright yellow grains onto his plate.

'Thank you, it's amazing, we'll have to come back,' Matt said.

There was a silence. Elizabeth's face warmed. She could not tell whether he had said 'I'll have to come back' or 'we'll have to come back', but it didn't matter. At that moment everything was perfect. She could feel the unmistakable flicker of nerves in her stomach, but despite them she could relax with Matt. It was not dread, it was the caution of new optimism. He did not seem to be intimidated by her, although he had a bashful, considerate air. She basked in the moment.

The waiter brought two dessert menus and placed them in Elizabeth and Matt's hands. The long, plastic menus had large photos of the options. Matt went for pistachio ice cream, and Elizabeth chose tropical fruit salad, the perfect follow-up to the spicy main course.

'Could I take a cup of tea as well, please?' Matt asked.

'Of course, sir,' the waiter said.

In the background, intricate Indian violin music had started playing on the sound system.

'Do you ever feel like you want a moment to just go on lasting and not end, as if you're content, and you don't want life to move on, because it can only go downhill?' Elizabeth asked.

'Pretty deep. Yeah, I do,' he agreed. 'When I left home and moved in with my brother, sorted out the room, and we sat down that night and ordered Pizza Hut.'

'Nice. So you were happy because your life was moving on?' she asked.

'I was happy that it had reached that point. I'd made it in a very small way, but sometimes that means everything.'

'I know what you mean. That's how I felt when I got the call from the airline telling me I got this job.' She raised her eyebrows. 'I was in Boots. Sad but true, that was one of those moments for me.'

Matt beamed.

'Are you saying you don't want *this* moment to end?' he asked carefully.

'Maybe,' she replied. Her heart had been pounding, and she now became aware of it. 'I once had a date with a Scottish guy who kept updating me on the progress of the date *during* the date,' she said.

Matt snorted in amusement and the tension was broken.

'It's reassuring to think I could never be that bad! Anyway, that's nothing: one of my female friends at college had a first date with this guy she met online, and she wanted to look her best. So she thought she'd try out her new colour contact lenses,' he explained.

'So far, so good,' Elizabeth said.

'So they went to a small bar in Tower Hill, small but still a bit dressy, and she liked it and thought everything was going well. She was a bit conscious about her weight back then, but she thought she was dressed well for the occasion, you know, in vertical stripes to play down the love handles.'

Elizabeth nodded.

'The problem was, one of her contacts had come a bit loose, and slipped halfway down her eye. She had no idea, because they'd been itching anyway, and she wasn't used to wearing them.'

Elizabeth bit her bottom lip.

'So they were sitting in the bar with their glasses of wine, everything was going well, and there was a lull in the conversation, so they both checked their phones. The guy put his phone in his pocket after sending a quick text,' Matt said.

He took a sip of tea for dramatic effect.

'So, then what happened?'

'Her phone buzzed right away and the guy's face just dropped - he suddenly looked mortified. She read the message she'd just received: 'Mate, I can't do this date, the girl's got a fucked up eye'. He thought he was texting one of his friends and didn't check the recipient, easily done.'

'Whoa,' Elizabeth mouthed.

'So he just stood up and started running away.'

'What? He ran away? He just left her on her own?'

'He literally just got up and ran away,' Matt chuckled. 'When you think about it, you can't salvage a situation like that.'

'That's hilarious, oh dear.'

'Well, what could he do? At least she could see the funny side! The moral is, stay away from colour contacts,' he said.

'Yeah, just be yourself! I'll never go near them after hearing that,' she laughed. 'Or you know, just no phones on dates. What's the worst date *you've* been on apart from Angela?' she asked. 'I'm joking, of course.'

'I've never actually had a bad date, the only problems were that it was never the right person, or maybe I wasn't the right person,' he said.

'I see. I don't mean to pry, but apart from Angela, have you dated anyone else from work?' she asked.

'No, I haven't. I've come close a couple of times but it's a risky idea. We don't have a normal job... by any means,' he said.

'No flings downroute?' she asked.

'Never. Not for me.'

'You're right, I guess. It isn't a normal job, Matt. I was thinking that with the size of the company you could probably be married to another crew member and never happen to fly together,' she said.

'Thinking about marriage already?' he joked. 'They do

have 'married rosters', I think that's what it's called, unless they rebranded it like they do with everything else' he said.

'So the couple can avoid each other, right?'

Matt nodded sarcastically, and sipping the last of the green ice cream from his spoon he stirred two sugar cubes into his tea.

Outside the sun had disappeared and the traffic had quietened.

'I never liked Hounslow at night,' Elizabeth reflected.

'I don't blame you, but it's like everything else, it has its moments.'

He put his hand on hers and she allowed it to rest there. His touch was warm and comforting, and Elizabeth felt at complete ease.

When they got back to the house, the kitchen and garden were empty and the house was very quiet. Paul came out of his room.

'Hey, guys,' he whispered, 'Angela and Nicko have gone to the Windsor Castle Pub to see Abbalicious, I'm no great Abba fan, though.'

'Abbalicious? I don't think we'll be joining them! We just had an amazing meal,' Elizabeth said.

'Really great stuff, thanks for the recommendation,' Matt said.

'Nice, nice. Well I'm just watching a TV series, I won't keep you. There are cookies in the fridge, help yourself,' he said, and returned to his room with a box of Maltesers from his cupboard.

'Want to see my room?' Elizabeth asked.

'Sure,' Matt said.

In her room, she closed the door, and Matt looked around at everything. He smiled at Elizabeth as she opened the window slightly. She could tell that he was nervous, as she felt *she* should be. But now she was calm. This was the first time in a long time that she could say she was starting to have promising feelings for another person. There was a magnetic pull that was utterly compelling, and she felt that Matt was so unique - she just knew that he could be someone special. It all felt so natural.

'Elizabeth,' he started.

'I don't think we should say any more,' she told him, stepping closer.

As she said this she put her hand on his face gently and he glowed.

'I want you,' he whispered.

They drew closer and their lips met. Elizabeth was breathing deeply through her nose, her hands grasped his, her heart started to pound again, and as he moved his lips she was swept away.

* * *

'So did you or didn't you?' Angela asked as she burst into Elizabeth's room the following day.

'Oh come in, it's not like I'm busy or anything,' Elizabeth replied, putting down a ringbinder full of revision notes.

'Spill the beans!' Angela rasped.

'It was a very good date,' Elizabeth admitted.

'I'm pleased for you!' Angela laughed. 'It sounds a lot more exciting than my date with him,' she added.

'It wasn't exciting exactly, I wouldn't put it in those words, but there was... a chemistry there,' Elizabeth said in an attempt to play things down.

'Aw, I'm really pleased for you. Work people, though. Are you sure it's a good idea, babe? Well, at least it's not one of the pilots, that would be...'

Elizabeth started to think back to what had happened with Tim and her stomach tightened slightly.

'Matt is good for you,' Angela said.

'And I think I'm maybe a good match for him,' Elizabeth suggested.

'It sucks that you're going to Bishkek tomorrow, just as the passion gets heated up!'

'I'm sure when we do have a second date the chemistry will still be there, I don't know why I didn't have more to do with him on the Agadir trip. He's...' she started in spite of herself.

'I told you! I was onto him before you! I admit, he has a charm,' Angela whispered in case Nicko, who was still in her room, might overhear.

'Yeah, something like that. There's something going on and I'm happy we clicked.'

'So tell me more: did he rock your world?' Angela asked gesturing at the bed.

Elizabeth's face flushed.

'Not in the way you're suggesting,' Elizabeth said.

'I'll take that as a resounding yes,' Angela finished with a wink, leaving to answer Nicko who had started calling out for her from her room.

Elizabeth thought back to the previous night and was filled with optimism. She went to the kitchen and bumped into Paul who needed help making some cupcakes.

20

'How are we going to do the service?' Evie asked.

There were three cabin crew in the rear galley: Evie, Elizabeth and Doris. In business class, Donato, the supervisor, was working alongside two other crew members.

'Let's do a drinks round first, do a mini clear-in, and then the hot food with wines and drinks on top, bread basket *with* the food, then tea and coffee by hand, top-ups by hand, if we all agree?' Evie said.

The other two did not want to contradict her. They had just taken off, but the boss had emerged.

'No problem with that,' Doris said in monotone.

'Cool,' Elizabeth said.

Doris was about fifty and seemed to be on edge. She had bleached blond hair which was kept back by a navy blue scrunchie, and she had dark blue eyeshadow which struck Elizabeth as very eighties, yet still elegant.

'Do you want to split up into three, and then we can meet in the middle?' Elizabeth asked. 'I'm quite fast.'

'Yes, and don't forget the sour cream pretzels,' Evie said.

Evie was making herself look busy with the ovens as she spoke, checking the temperature, and Elizabeth and Doris started to stuff the tiny bags of pretzels into the top drawers of the bar trolleys.

'Dry heat will do the job on the kosher hot bits, I think. I don't want any food getting cold, you know what they're like.'

'Diet Coke is the most popular on this route, isn't it?' Doris asked her.

'They always ask for Diet Sprite, but we ain't got it, so give them diet lemonade or Diet Coke. The only other diet stuff is slimline tonic but nobody drinks that crap,' she said and pulled a disgusted face.

'Got it,' Elizabeth said.

'Wait, let me put some Diet Cokes aside for us,' she said placing twelve cans in the side cupboard, 'there'll be none left for us at this rate.'

The flight to Bishkek was jam packed, and there were a lot of children and teenagers on board.

'Fill half that drawer with Coke cans, that's all the kids drink, and don't waste ice on them,' Evie ordered.

'I don't see why they need three crew up there in business, they only have, what, twelve passengers? That's four each, it's ridiculous,' Evie proclaimed.

'Yep, but I'd still rather be back here slumming it in cattle class. There's less fuss,' Doris said.

'Right, no fuss.' Evie looked her up and down. 'I'm a Ghanaian girl, we're down to earth,' she said squeezing handfuls of pretzel packets into the top drawer of the drinks trolley.

'Shall we bother with tea and coffee with this first drinks round?' Elizabeth asked.

'Nah, hot drinks on demand, don't worry about the

service standards,' Evie said.

'I'll go up first,' said Doris. She looked panic-stricken and took the brakes off the trolley before speeding up the aisle.

'That's it, get out there before they all start wanting the toilets, girl,' Evie called to her, finishing off an ice cube. 'Smiles in the aisles!'

'Why do you eat ice?' Elizabeth asked.

'Nothing on here is clean. I never have and never will go near an economy toilet,' she replied.

'But it's part of our checks,' Elizabeth said.

'Not part of *my* checks. You don't know what you're going to catch in there. It's disgusting. In Freetown they use an old T-shirt to wipe down the toilet, then use the same thing to clean the seats and the tray tables, that's if they can be bothered. If you tell them not to do it, they just laugh at you. I eat ice because the bacteria have been killed off by freezing them,' she added.

'You need to use the gin to clean the galley tops too, but they'll never tell you that in training. At least three Gordon's,' she went on, wearing a frown. 'Right, let's get on with it, the sooner it's done, the sooner I can look forward to Bishkek. I'm famous over there, you'll see!'

As soon as Doris had reached the curtain divider, Evie looked at Elizabeth with a skeptical expression on her face.

'She's a classic flapper. I knew from the word go. I can't stand flapping,' she said. 'You'll see, I know the type.'

'She's okay. There's no 'I' in team,' Elizabeth said in an

ironic tone pulling her cart out slowly.

Evie pushed out her front teeth to make a goofy face, and made a mock gesture of sincere nodding.

'Very fresh from recurrent, I see.'

'I'm just twelve months in, is it obvious?' Elizabeth asked.

'I've been around long enough, I know it all,' she said. 'I'll stay down here near the end, so if you need anything run up from the galley, just press a call bell,' she added.

'Sure,' Elizabeth said.

'I like you, Elizabeth, you're just chill.'

The passengers in the last row were following the conversation.

'You can help me diffuse the flapping,' she added.

Elizabeth started at one of the overwing emergency exit rows. A young couple were first.

'Would you like any drinks?' Elizabeth asked handing out two packs of pretzels with branded napkins, the airline's logo facing the passengers.

'Two tomato juice,' the man said.

* * *

'Look how everyone stares at me,' Evie said.

And it was true. As they walked down the shopping

street in the centre of town almost everyone was looking at Evie as if she had just stepped off a spaceship.

'It's a bit of a bleak place isn't it?' she asked.

Elizabeth had been noticing the same thing. It was very cold in Bishkek despite it being summer, and things seemed to be incredibly spread out. There were Soviet style buildings everywhere and the overall impression was of a city that had once been austere and still lacked the confidence to install anything to offer visual relief. Grey dominated, and a handful of western designer brand shops had been grafted on recently and unconvincingly by the looks of things.

'Are you hungry?' Evie asked.

'A little. What's the food like here?' she asked.

'There's a place up here I've been to a few times,' she replied.

They walked into a large restaurant which had raw kebabs lined up behind a glass counter. They took a table near the stage where a man was singing a ballad in English on a karaoke machine. A waiter came over.

'Hello,' Evie started. 'We take rice, you know, rice,' she said. 'Rice and kebab good? Good,' she said making gestures with her hands.

'They don't speak English,' she explained to Elizabeth picking up a breadstick from the table. 'What do you have when you get back?' she asked.

'Recurrent,' Elizabeth replied.

'That's life,' Evie shrugged. 'You have to do it,' she

added.

'Yep, first time,' Elizabeth said.

Evie looked around at the restaurant. Elizabeth had worried that she would be bossy, but Evie had relaxed somewhat downroute.

'What do you think of the whole thing, then?' she asked.

'Of Bishkek?' Elizabeth asked.

'No, of flying,' Evie replied.

'I enjoy it. I do enjoy it. As repetitive as it can be,' she said.

'I've been doing this shit for over ten years,' Evie let out. 'It's not something you should get used to otherwise you end up not being able to do anything else.'

Elizabeth didn't know what to say so there was a silence.

'Don't listen to me,' Evie continued. 'It's putting my eldest through private school, but it's bloody hard work and you get stuck. You've got to do what's in your heart. You're young enough to follow your dreams.'

Elizabeth smiled. They shared a salad and Evie had her rice and kebab which she picked at suspiciously at first.

'Bacteria,' she explained.

Evie told Elizabeth about her disastrous first marriage to a minicab driver.

'The bastard bled me dry, financially AND emotionally. I'm done with men,' she said.

'So... You're a lesbian now?' Elizabeth asked.

'No! I'm just done with men. Waste of time, most of them. You must know what I mean?'

'Kind of. Can't tar them all with the same brush, though.'

'You might change your mind when you get to my age,' Evie said.

They split the bill and looked around in a single floor shopping centre afterwards which was tucked behind a massive public park. The place was very empty and the few people that were there stared at Evie. Some of them even stopped walking to stand and stare.

'Fame,' she said.

'It's crazy,' Elizabeth said. 'It's like they're watching a freak show.'

'You get used to it,' Evie said. 'You can get used to anything.'

21

Angela and Elizabeth had been assigned different groups for the recurrent, although she was happy to see that a familiar face, Fiona, was in her group. Each group's classroom had a smartboard at the front and chairs with individual wooden tables arranged in a circle. There were office chairs with wheels for the trainers. The training centre had lots of small classrooms, and in the middle of the building a massive atrium containing mock-ups of parts of aircraft with inflated slides, and life-size walk-through reconstructions of survival situations such as desert islands and forests.

'Right, a warm welcome to everyone. I'm Summer, your primary instructor. I hope you've all been studying your emergency equipment location diagrams - on all aircraft!'

The group groaned collectively.

'Because that's what we're testing this evening first off the bat, to get it out of the way. Your second actual exam is tomorrow afternoon in this room at four sharp, and that's on the topic we're covering after the hazmat stuff: Boeing 767 standard operating procedures. If you're late, that's an automatic fail,' she paused for dramatic effect and looked around at the group waiting for it to sink in.

Is she joking? Elizabeth thought. But she had been in the company long enough now to know that this was not a joke.

Punctuality was taken incredibly seriously, and her face sank as she envisioned yet another night of late study and an early morning following the sleepless night.

'Just chill babe, you're worse than me!' Fiona said under her breath. 'You're allowed to get some of them wrong.'

Fiona was sitting between Elizabeth and an older man called Karl who was from Switzerland. He turned to Fiona.

'Do they think we're children? It's so patronising,' he whispered shaking his head.

'What I don't get is the uniforms they have on,' she whispered back. 'They don't ever actually fly, they just spend their days telling other people how to do it!'

'As you can see from the outline that's being passed round, wet drills are tomorrow morning, so we suggest you bring in light clothes to change into, and nothing that turns see-through, ladies and gentleman!' Summer began. 'We'll be taking a coach to West Drayton Pool, so obviously don't be late: those guys are doing us a *huge* favour by letting us book the pool for these training events, so please be as respectful and polite as we know you are because there will probably be members of the public there at the same time as us doing their morning swims. Oh, and remember to bring a towel.'

Karl looked at Fiona and Elizabeth as if these comments vindicated what he had said, and Elizabeth unconsciously curled the side of her mouth into a snarl. Fiona looked at her nails.

'The final exams are all computerised, and when we say exam conditions that means no speaking or communication of any kind. All mobiles must be switched off, and anyone with a phone ringing or beeping during the recurrent will have one warning,' she said.

'Summer, what happens if you go to second warning?'

someone asked.

'You'll have to attend a meeting with your line manager to discuss your position with the airline. We are taking this very seriously. Of course, anyone can make a mistake, we all have our bad days. But look guys, we're here to get you through this, and we'll give you all the help you need.' Her tone lacked any trace of sincerity. 'But after that *first* warning, it's really not going to be acceptable. That means punctuality, phones, and talking. Does everyone understand?'

'Yes,' they recited.

'Great, now that we've gotten all *that* business out of the way, let's introduce ourselves and then we can get cracking on with our first *revision* topic which is easy-peasy, I'm sure you all agree, and that is hazardous materials! We'll be doing a simple open-book test, so don't bother trying to memorise loads of information.' Summer pushed a wisp of hair back behind her ear.

There was a sigh of relief from the group.

'Okay, first thing's first, does anyone nice and confident want to go first and introduce themselves to the group?' she asked.

Fiona stood up.

'My name's Fiona, ex-Concorde,' she started.

'Hello, Fiona!' Summer recited.

'Very nervous, hate wet drills, hate swimming pools - sure I'm not the only one - and I dread the exams every year, especially bloody av-med' she said.

Summer gave her a polite smile. The other trainer, a fresh-faced blond man called Christophe, chimed in.

'We try to make it all as user-friendly as possible,' he said. 'You work with us, and we'll get through it together,' he said holding up his hand and crossing his fingers.

His speech, like Summer's, was infused with pure fakeness, and he bore a smile that was far too sincere.

His mouth has been trained to behave that way, Elizabeth thought. His face was so cartoonishly sweet and innocent.

'I know I've been in this game for years, but I still lose sleep over the exams,' Fiona finished, sitting back down.

'It's not a counselling session,' someone muttered.

Fiona was oblivious.

'We all know exactly how you feel,' Christophe went on, 'but by this time next week you'll wonder what all the fuss was about back out there online!' His face switched to serious mode. 'End of the day, we're here to help you be the best cabin crew you can be out there in the sky so you can keep everyone safe.'

When the introductions came to a close, he picked up a pile of handouts and started distributing them to the group. Summer took a seat next to a computer.

'Now, does anyone here actually have any experience with hazardous materials?' he asked.

A young, very tanned, woman called Vanya put her hand up.

'Ooh, let's hear what happened,' he said.

'Well I was taking hot pa-a-asta from the oven. The oven gloves were too big. You know I have very small fingers.' She held her hands up and some people in the group nodded. 'So I used that - you know - blue paper roll stuff to make like a pad.'

Christophe hummed.

'And this pa-a-asta was so hot that I dropped one of them, and the sauce was on my uniform, and I got it all over my fingers. I had to clean up this whole mess from, like, the galley worktop, from the floor, from my shirt... I was like *oh my God*.'

Christophe stared at her without comprehension.

A grey-haired man called Mark came to the rescue.

'That's not hazardous materials, hun, that's just you dropping the food.'

The group laughed long and hard, and Vanya turned from orange to red. Elizabeth squirmed. Christophe smiled quizzically.

'Let's move on to my list, shall we? Please turn to the first handout,' he said.

Looking down at the pages on his mini-desk, and frowning under concentration, Karl bit a fingernail and snorted.

'Here we go,' Fiona whispered.

* * *

The morning was a torture that dragged on. During the lunch break, Angela paid for her lunch and walked with her tray over to Elizabeth's table. She sat next to her.

'How's it going?' she asked, piercing her Capri-Sun with the straw.

'Not bad, hazardous materials done, we all passed.'

'Same here. Shocker.'

'When are your wet drills?' she asked.

'I think we're doing them with your group, actually, tomorrow morning.'

'Yeah, 767 stuff this afternoon with the exam tomorrow afternoon. I just want to cry,' Elizabeth said.

'You'll be fine, just take your time, because the computer's unforgiving,' Angela said.

'Thanks, but it's going to be a late night.'

'Poor thing. Your late night tête-à-têtes making cupcakes with Paul will have to take a break,' she said.

Elizabeth paused before she replied. She sensed some anger behind the comment.

'Is it my fault that you've moved Nicko in? You're constantly locked up with him in your room, you were welcome to join us,' she said. 'I'm not blaming you, but we hardly ever see you.'

After a noticeable pause, Angela replied.

'You wouldn't know how it is in a distance relationship. I

have to make the most of my time with him,' she said.

'Angela, it's not a problem, but Paul and I have become quite close. I *like* hanging out with him'

'Hanging out?' Angela smirked.

'What? It's not like that, he's fun to spend time with. He's engaged to a girl back home in Poland in any case.'

'It's not like you've never been the other woman,' Angela said.

Elizabeth was silent.

'Sorry, I didn't mean that.'

'There's nothing going on with me and Paul, and if I'd known that you-know-who was married, I would never have... You *know* that.'

Elizabeth felt mentally exhausted, and now this tiresome quarrel with Angela over nothing. She had no mental energy spare for bickering. She stood up without saying anything and emptied what was left on her tray in the rubbish bag. She walked to the exit to go outside for some fresh air.

'What's gotten into her?' Angela said to some others from her group who were joining the table.

As Elizabeth was leaving the canteen, Fiona bumped into her.

'Hey, hun!' she said.

'Oh hi, Fiona,' Elizabeth said.

'I'm going for a ciggie, join me?' she asked.

'I quit a long time ago. But I'll join you, sure, let's go.'

They stood in the smoking area: a small part of the forecourt sectioned off with a clear plastic shelter and tall cement ashtrays. Fiona was drinking a can of Diet Coke through a straw, her cigarette in the other hand. Elizabeth missed the ritual of smoking.

'You look more traumatised than *me*, what's up?' she asked Elizabeth.

'Just the stress of this thing. I think we're all on edge,' she replied.

'It's only day one, you need to take a chill pill. I've given up on getting a normal night's sleep, but we all know that in a few weeks when we're back out online this is going to be like a distant memory. Life goes on, that's my mantra,' she said.

'I just feel like I've been shut in that classroom all day. And it's only twelve-thirty,' Elizabeth said.

Fiona chuckled.

'I can't wait for it to be over,' she added with impotence.

A group of young looking trainees passed by the entrance.

'Fresh meat,' Fiona said.

'They must be here for initial,' Elizabeth said.

'Yeah. It seems like yesterday, I was up there on the Concorde, glamming it, fresh-faced. Now look at me,' she said scrunching up her face. 'I heard on Galley FM that your mum's a plastic surgeon,' she added.

'That's true, but she only does burns work,' she said.

Fiona picked up her lighter and mimed burning her face off.

'You still look as fresh as ever, don't beat yourself up,' Elizabeth said.

'The neck doesn't lie,' Fiona said, putting her hand on her throat.

'What cream do you use?' Elizabeth asked.

'The Clinique ones from the Duty Free cart, but there's only so much you can expect a cream to do.'

The rest of the day went as slowly as the morning and Angela seemed to be avoiding her in the breaks. *Well let her*, she thought. Elizabeth only had studying to look forward to by the time she arrived back home.

The air in the train carriage was stuffy and the sunlight made everything look yellow and somehow reminded Elizabeth of being back in primary school. A pregnant woman came on when the train stopped at a station and Elizabeth offered up her seat, but the woman refused politely.

She was dipping into the agony aunt book for light relief and still had quite a chunk of problems left. When she reached the house she took a hot shower to freshen up, and sat at her desk, trying to gather her focus.

* * *

The next day, wet drills were scheduled. As Elizabeth and Angela's groups were taking the tests at the same time, they had to take the same coach from the training centre to the local pool at 9am. For some reason, Angela had sat far away from Elizabeth on the coach.

She sensed that something was wrong, but could not put her finger on it. Her behaviour seemed to be an overreaction, and in any case, with the stress of being assessed and the lack of sleep, Elizabeth decided not to worry too much about it.

When the groups assembled next to the pool in their swimming costumes plus some loose fitting 'normal' clothes over the top of them, Summer read out the instructions very carefully over the moaning about the smell of chlorine and the effect it would have on hair.

'Guys, the first thing we need you to do is tread water for one minute without holding onto the side, and please no actual swimming. Only treading! Please enter the pool,' she said with a serious look on her made-up face as many of the crew started to scream at how cold the water was.

'Nicko is staying for another two days... if that's okay with certain people,' Angela said to Elizabeth.

'Oh, good morning, how have you been?' she replied, treading the water.

Summer was holding a digital stopwatch but kept being distracted by the clipboard she was juggling which had instructions on it and a list of the two crew groups' names. She looked dismayed.

'I wasn't trying to be rude, but if you have a problem

with...' Angela began.

'I don't have a problem with Nicko, there's no problem,' she replied.

'So it's all in my head?' Angela asked shuffling up close to Elizabeth.

'What is this really about? I couldn't think what the issue is. Is it Matt? Are you jealous?' she asked.

As she said this she had unintentionally gestured in the water and splashed some into Angela's face.

Angela flushed red and her face screwed into an angry scowl. Suddenly her arms sprang from the water and she submerged Elizabeth by her shoulders. Some of the crew screamed.

'Stop her!' Summer cried.

Elizabeth came up gasping for air.

'She trying to drown me! Help!' she called out.

Angela was pulled off by two women as Summer shook her head not really knowing what to do.

The other swimmers, a handful of elderly people who had come for their daily dip looked utterly confused. Angela swam to the edge and got out of the pool heading to the changing rooms her face still bearing a look of fury.

'Are you okay, honey? I saw everything, make sure you breathe!' Fiona said.

'I'm okay. I think I said the wrong thing,' Elizabeth gasped.

* * *

After a meeting with their line managers who seemed annoyed at the inconvenience to their schedules, Angela and Elizabeth were suspended from duties for one week, which struck Elizabeth as unfair - after all, she had not done anything wrong. Angela was given a warning and a note in her file. The outcome was that if she received any other warnings for behavioural issues, she would be fired. This did strike Elizabeth as fair despite the fact that she had pleaded for the managers not to punish her friend. Outside the airline's headquarters, they stood at the bus stop waiting to leave.

'For what it's worth, I'm sorry,' Angela said.

'You're sorry?' Elizabeth replied.

'I honestly am sorry. I lost it. Maybe I am a bit jealous. You and Matt seem so happy together, and you haven't done anything wrong. In fact, you stuck up for me in there. I appreciate it,' she said.

'You have Nicko,' Elizabeth said. 'You love him.'

'Do I? Sometimes I think we're just a typical co-dependent couple. We barely have anything in common,' she said.

'You seem happy... most of the time,' Elizabeth said.

'I didn't want to drown you,' Angela said very carefully.

'I know, but it came out of the blue. I didn't mean to

splash you,' she replied.

'I'm surprised they didn't fire me on the spot. Thanks for not making a big thing about this. I suppose our friendship is... over,' she said.

Elizabeth was silent for a few moments.

'I understand. Don't worry about it,' she offered.

'So you mean...'

'I mean don't worry about it. Let's let bygones be bygones. We can move past it,' Elizabeth said. 'It's just childish anyway, we should both know better.'

Angela's eyes started to tear up. She hugged Elizabeth.

'You're one in a million. I'm lucky to know you, you know that?' she said.

'Yeah, yeah, let's not go over the top. Friends again,' she said.

'I'm so sorry all of this happened,' Angela said.

'On the bright side, it gives us more time to study for the new recurrent.'

22

She was trying to stay awake in spite of the stinging feeling in her face and pain in her back. It was as though Elizabeth's entire body was rebelling against her. Her body *hated* her for staying awake and forcing it to keep going.

'I must stay awake,' she repeated to herself, 'just one more day'.

She went down to the kitchen to boil the kettle for a second strong, black coffee. When she got back to her desk, she started to line up the pile of manuals and organise the bundles of notepaper into stacks, according to when the new schedule of when exams were due to take place. University had been hard work, at times unbearably hard, but in comparison this was terrible. It was the short time frame and the high stakes if she failed to memorise any given piece of information correctly.

She deliberately breathed in and out slowly and took a sip of the coffee. Her legs trembled in slow motion. She had to get organised.

Glancing at her phone she saw that it was almost three o'clock already. In a few hours it would be light again, so there was no time to lose. Sitting there at the desk cramming, she thought back to something that had happened in her last months of university. The course of events that in fact had led her to be sitting there putting herself through this into the early hours of the morning.

* * *

Luke stopped walking when he noticed her and looked her over with a confused face.

'When did you take that up, Elizabeth?' he asked.

She looked up. He was referring to the cigarette in her hand.

'About a year ago.'

'A very bad habit,' he said, and went on into the building with a smile on his face.

The day had been slow, and she was taking a break from her solitary revision session in the library. Luke - Dr Pearce - had always been friendly with her, but she suspected he did not take her as seriously as a student as he did the others for some reason.

She had the impression that she had never done enough background reading or completed her assignments in enough detail to mark herself out as fully dedicated to the discipline of history - at least not enough to stand out from the rest of her cohort. In any case, she had come in on one of her free days to prepare. It would be exam time soon and she wanted to avoid any panic setting in by getting ready ahead of time.

Luke usually seemed amused. He was a junior professor of history, of medium height, but had a solid, sturdy build, and Elizabeth was sure that outside of lecturing, he lifted weights or did some kind of sport. He seemed aloof, but a little smug. She was certain that he smoked himself, and his comment was just as much self-criticism as criticism directed at her.

How old was he? Elizabeth never found out, but he was the young one in the faculty and stood out - he showed no signs of going bald or grey. At what point did she decide that she liked him, and that she wanted him? Was it during a seminar? Was it just something that had always been there in the air, just existing in the background?

She was certain he would never have pursued her, if only because it was against his professional ethics. That meant pushing the reservations from her mind, and deciding to actively put in the groundwork.

Although it took a long time for the relationship to begin, Elizabeth had practically moved in with Luke in his small flat packed with books in Mile End by the time the next term was almost over. He enjoyed taking her out and showing her off, although never when university people were involved.

When the flattery of being a young status symbol wore off, Elizabeth began to feel more and more objectified, as if she were a commodity rather than a girlfriend. Things came to their lowest point when he took her on a short break in Nice, and they began to bicker on the flight back. At one point he growled at her, 'I do NOT show you off.'

As Elizabeth sat in her seat for the landing she felt trapped, stressed and miserable. Although she had once entertained going into academia, when she thought of Luke's life she began to see that path unravel for her. All she could imagine was being a female version of Luke, maybe even with a toyboy she felt insecure about and an untidy flat in the East End full of old books.

'Are you okay?' the hostess asked her.

'Oh, yes, I'm fine,' Elizabeth replied looking up at the glamorous stranger in a blue hat.

As she walked off she overheard her saying to her colleague, 'she must be afraid of flying'.

Afraid of flying, no. Fed up with the course her life was taking.

It was then that she decided to try out new things and made a list on a napkin where she listed the idea of flying after graduating. The end of the final year of her degree was filled with stress and having an ex teaching her added to it. His new policy seemed to be simply ignoring her, in fact he never made eye contact. She started to eat more than usual. She started to gain weight. Then there was Peter. He had been wonderful and loving, and they rushed headfirst into their romance.

Elizabeth looked down into her desk drawer and stared at the napkin, as good as new, sitting among the perfume bottles, pens and post-its. She had kept it for its sentimental value.

Although the break up had been mutual, she did still miss Peter. She did not miss Luke, but reflected that he had been instrumental in the direction her life had taken. For better or worse.

* * *

At half past four in the morning, Elizabeth decided to stop torturing herself and allow herself some sleep. The next day she sat a battery of exams. By the time the last one came around, everyone in the group was itching to get out of the place.

'Congratulations, Elizabeth,' Summer said very woodenly. 'Marks in the 80 and 90 percents. We're glad that all that *unpleasantness* the first time around didn't phase you.'

She had passed the recurrent.

'Thank you, Summer. Maybe I'll see you on a flight soon,' Elizabeth said as Summer took the recurrent attestation document she had just signed and was putting it into a folder. If the comment had come off as bitchy, she no longer cared.

Summer gave her a wide, fake grin and Elizabeth flushed with happiness. She hoped that now her life would regain a semblance of normality.

23

Matt opened his eyes and lucidity started to return. He was next to Elizabeth in her soft, white bed. He looked over at the wall, behind which he could hear a muffled conversation. Elizabeth was still asleep.

He stroked her thigh, and she roused.

'Good morning,' she said in a high pitched voice.

'Good morning!' he replied, and kissed her cheek.

The conversation in the next room fell silent. Then, a few seconds later, the sound of the bed squeaking in rhythm and the bed head tapping the wall started.

Elizabeth felt embarrassed. She looked at Matt. They both snickered.

'Shh, they might hear,' he whispered.

'Well it doesn't seem like they care about us hearing, does it?' she replied.

Elizabeth stood up and went over to the window to open it fully. The gardens outside were bathed in bright sunlight, and fresh air floated into the room.

'What shall we do today?' she asked. 'I don't know about you, but I'm happy to stay in.'

'We can just have an easy day if you want,' he replied, putting his hands behind his head.

Elizabeth sat on the side of the bed and Matt returned his

hand to her thigh.

'I'm going to have a quick shower,' she said as she stroked the soft fair hairs on the back of his hand.

She leaned over and gave him a peck on the cheek. In the shower, she used the cedar shampoo she had discovered in Tehran and tea tree oil shower gel from the Body Shop. She loved the aroma of the two mingling together and she inhaled it deeply. After drying herself, she changed into a t-shirt and shorts and went back into her room. Matt was waiting.

He lifted the t-shirt slightly and started rubbing his face slowly on her stomach.

'It tickles!' she said, reacting to his dark stubble, but she made no effort to stop him.

He wrapped his long arms around her body and she eased into position.

'You smell amazing,' he whispered.

'Thanks.'

'I should probably have a shower myself.'

A moment after he said that, the sound of the bathroom door creaking shut and the latch sliding across came through the wall followed by LBC on the radio and Nicko's electric toothbrush.

'Unlucky,' Elizabeth said.

She stroked Matt's hair and he started to lick her midriff delicately with the tip of his tongue. She tried her best not to giggle. He cupped her chest under the t-shirt and she started to stroke the back of his neck pulling off the t-shirt with the other hand and easing herself onto his rising head allowing him to nestle into her breasts.

Suddenly Matt rose and towered above her. She pulled down his boxer shorts and he breathed out loudly. It was the start of an enjoyable day off.

24

Elizabeth noticed that the City Mall in Beirut was very similar to how she remembered it when she had been there on the trip with Christine, and on the whole very similar to the City Mall in Amman; a little brighter perhaps, and Jordan *was* a little more rough around the edges. Elizabeth wanted to get Matt a gift, so she decided to search for one in a shop that sold handmade soap with herbal ingredients on the ground floor. The woman behind the counter spoke to her in lightly-accented English.

'Is it a gift? Man or woman?'

'It's a gift for a special man,' Elizabeth replied.

The woman stood up and held out a small cube of purple soap that was wrapped in crepe paper for Elizabeth to smell, a mixture of lavender and mint.

'Masculine,' the woman said.

'It's very nice, which other ones do you have for men?'

The woman pointed at a section of the shop that was lit up with blue and purple bulbs. The gift boxes filled the lower shelves. Elizabeth noticed that the woman was wearing a gold necklace and began to wonder if jewellery would make a better gift. She decided against it since Matt had never worn any accessories in the times she had seen him outside of work. The woman sat back down behind the counter and went back to adding up lists of figures in a notebook while Elizabeth browsed.

A gift at this stage in the relationship was difficult to judge. She did not want to seem clingy and run the risk of freaking him out, but at the same time she wanted to give him something meaningful to show she had thought about him while they were away from each other and that this was special.

She settled on a green men's gift box that contained lime shower gel, face cream and a small eau de toilette. The price was not too bad, but it was not cheap either, and after the shop assistant had gift wrapped the box in shiny gold paper, Elizabeth thought it looked perfect. A familiar voice emerged from behind her back.

'Who's *that* for, darling?'

It was Fiona.

'Hey! I didn't know you were over here,' Elizabeth said.

'I'm an international woman of mystery! That looks like something for a significant person,' she hinted.

'You got me. I hope I don't scare him off.'

'Oh it *is* a boy then. Do go on!'

'I don't want to jinx it,' she replied.

'Hm, I see,' she said, pausing in hope of further information.

'Yeah, I don't want to say.'

Elizabeth had already learned a lesson about gossip.

'Fair enough, I hope he likes it, whoever the lucky chap is. This shop smells like absolute heaven.'

'I love it. Are you here on the five day?'

'I'm never that lucky. We're going back early tomorrow,

but I had to get away from that hotel, or else I turn into Jack Nicholson. The captain's an absolute arsehole, too. On the way over, he left his used tray out on the galley top, took some Pringles, and then disappeared back to his box.'

'Do you fancy going for a walk outside? It's not too hot now,' Elizabeth suggested.

'Sure,' Fiona said, and they walked towards the front exits, shopping in hand.

Outside the mall, the traffic was noisy and the pavement thinned into a narrow walkway.

'Let's head up this way, we can go to the Armenian Quarter.'

They came up to an area of the city with lots of small shops, and lining the roads were lean trees with puffy arrangements of leaves at the tops, and parked cars everywhere. The number of jewellery shops stood out, and Elizabeth and Fiona stopped from time to time to admire the window displays.

'Were you in a lot of trouble for the... 'incident'... during recurrent?' she asked.

'It wasn't as bad as I thought it would be. To be fair, it wasn't entirely Angela's fault. I shouldn't have lost my temper and provoked her like that. What did Summer say is the one thing you always have to be able to do in this job?'

'Keep a cool head you guys!' Fiona answered, mimicking Summer's simpering voice.

'Right. I really let myself down that day,' Elizabeth

added.

'You can't blame yourself for what happened, I probably would have gone off the deep end if I were in the same position you were: she had you under the water.'

'We both went off the deep end. Literally. I thought we were both going to get kicked out of the company for sure.'

'So what *was* the outcome?'

'We had to sit down and have a meeting with both of our managers. They wanted to know everything. In the end, we agreed to a sort of truce. But it's hard living there now, sharing a house with her. Neither of us can let bygones be bygones - not really, not fully.'

'You used to be best friends,' Fiona said sagely.

'Not best friends, but we were close. She was my best friend at work.'

'But you didn't think of moving?'

'It crossed my mind. It's easier to stay.'

'Well you're still friends. Time heals all wounds.'

'Let's hope so,' Elizabeth concluded.

25

Joggers trotted by, and behind them rowers glided past on the river, taking it in their stride. The whole atmosphere that afternoon was relaxed. Richmond was idyllic at that time of year. Matt and Elizabeth sat on the grass against an oak tree where they had been hugging for quite some time.

'We should probably...' Matt started.

'Yeah, let's get something to drink,' Elizabeth said.

They stood up and made their way over to a café that was not too busy and had seats and tables outside where they took a position facing the river. On the tabletops the wood was visibly worn and splintered in places; there was some old food, some crumbs, trapped in the surfaces. But the flawed and rustic look of the chairs and tables enhanced the surroundings - further up the river there were trendy, shiny modern restaurants, and even further up some new pubs and a vodka bar - but here the traditional ambiance imbued this nook on the bank with the perfect timeless quality, and it was enchanting.

'I was going to wait to give you this, but it seems like the right time,' Elizabeth hedged.

'Give me what? What is it?! You really didn't have to get me anything,' Matt said.

She took out the gold wrapped box and it shone in the sunlight.

'Hey!' he said.

'Go ahead, open it, I just hope it's your kind of thing.'

Matt held the box up to the side of his head and shook it lightly. He tore the side of the paper revealing the selection in the box and then paused. She noticed that he looked fairly taken aback. His eyes even appeared to be watery as he folded the torn wrapping paper up into a neat pile.

'Say something,' she said panicking.

'It's so thoughtful. I don't know what to say.'

'No big deal,' she said.

'Thank you so much,' he added and leaned over the table to kiss her.

The woman at the table next to them who had been pretending not to listen rolled her eyes and sipped her tea.

Elizabeth settled back in her seat to take in the scenery again. There were some moments that seemed to fit into the plan, if there was a plan. It felt as though everything was working out. Matt was sniffing the box, his cheeks dimpled from his uncontrollable grin, so Elizabeth giggled.

They each had a cappuccino and shared a piece of Victoria sponge cake, Elizabeth nibbling her portion and allowing Matt to take the majority.

'You think I eat a lot don't you?' Matt asked. 'And you're wondering how someone who eats this much could be not be fat.'

'It's because you have a fast metabolism.'

'It must be, because if you think of all the stuff I eat on flights, plus the takeaways, well...'

'You probably have a doppelgänger somewhere who can't shift any weight despite living off salad,' she said. 'You're definitely lucky, I hope you realise. Do you ever work out?'

'Hardly ever. If the hotel has a pool I normally do go for a swim, but apart from that it's not my thing, never was' he said. He stroked the back of her hand.

'I've been going to a kickboxing gym,' she said. 'Well, going *back* really.'

A group of ducks waddled past the table.

'They probably want some crumbs,' Elizabeth said.

'They're so cute,' Matt remarked.

He pulled out a camera with a big lens from his bag cautiously and lowered his shoulders to snap the ducks before putting the camera back satisfied.

'So what's it like, the gym?'

'It's small - for a kickboxing gym - but the two guys who run it are really nice. I'm glad I go there. It's in Euston, though, so it means going out of my way.'

'But didn't you say your parents *live* in Euston?' he asked.

'Yes, but... I don't always feel like dropping in,' she said.

'I understand.'

There was an awkward silence.

'Do you... think that you might want to meet up with them one of these days?' she asked.

The delivery of the question was tentative because it was so loaded. Was it too soon? Furthermore, she was not exactly relishing the idea of having Matt be subjected to her parents' scrutiny, but at the same time she knew he was someone different from her past boyfriends - it was inevitable that the meeting would take place at some point. It was inevitable that the scrutinisation would take place, too. Would Matt be put off by the idea?

'I'd love to!' he said. 'When do you want to go?'

'Give me a copy of your next month's roster, and I'll see when we can pop in for a quick visit,' she said.

'Sorted,' he said, lifting the last piece of cake to his mouth.

* * *

The door opened and Matt lifted the bunch of flowers up ready to hand them to Elizabeth's parents. A short lady opened the door.

'Hello!' she said.

'Kamusta na po kayo?' Elizabeth said.

'Hello, hello... I'm Carmen, so nice to meet you,' she laughed. 'Come in!'

'Nice to meet you,' said Matt, still clutching the upheld bunch.

'Your mother is a bit late. Do you want to have some drinks?'

'Erm, I'll just have a Coke, if you've got one?'

'Me, too,' said Elizabeth.

She turned to Matt.

'That's Carmen, she's been living with us since I was young,' she explained.

'Cool,' said Matt, trying to appear calm in spite of his nerves.

Elizabeth had noticed his nervousness - he wanted to make a good impression. He sat down stiffly on the sofa in the main room and gazed around at the paintings on the wall and the grand piano in the far corner which had tidy piles of sheet music on a table next to it.

'So do you speak...' he started.

'Tagalog? Just a few words. Carmen taught me the basics,' she replied.

Carmen came into the room.

'Here you are, if you want anything to eat before dinner let me know, I'm making you a special meal!' she said, smiling at Matt.

'Thank you,' he said.

The sound of keys in the door echoed in the long hallway.

'Mum's home,' Elizabeth said adjusting her top.

'You must be Matt! So nice to meet you, my dear, so nice' Yvonne effused.

'Nice to meet you, these are for you!' Matt said holding

out the flowers.

'Darling, you shouldn't have! Let me have Carmen put these in some water,' she replied.

Elizabeth flushed red - it was even more excruciating than she had imagined. Matt could instantly see the family resemblance. Yvonne's face was an older version of Elizabeth's, slightly more worn, but cast from the same mould.

'They're beautiful,' Yvonne added.

'Mrs Brown...'

'Please, call me Yvonne,' she interrupted. 'We're practically family now, Elizabeth has told me so much about you!' she said reaching out her left arm to hug Matt who obliged.

'Mum, don't embarrass me,' Elizabeth said.

'Don't be ridiculous, we're so happy you've finally brought someone back to *meet* us,' she intoned while sizing Matt up. 'I'll save the embarrassing mother stuff for later when we go through your baby pictures!'

Elizabeth put one hand on her forehead.

'Michael will be back a bit later, they're keeping him at the office. I don't know how he can stand it this late,' she added.

Carmen drifted in and took the flowers.

'Water,' she nodded to Yvonne.

'How long will dinner be, darling?' she asked.

'Give me half an hour,' Carmen replied.

'Superb. I'm absolutely starved,' she said. 'Matt, is it

okay if I call you Matt?'

'Matt's fine!' Elizabeth said.

Yvonne took a seat opposite the couple and leaned forward.

'Matt, are you a drinker?' she asked with a hint of suspicion.

'Not really. Well, what I mean is, only from time to time,' he replied.

'Superb! I've been waiting for an occasion to open a fantastic champagne, I didn't want it to go to waste. Carmen, we'll have the '43 with dinner. How exciting!'

Elizabeth was happy to see her mother in such a good mood, but at the same time she would have preferred a more down-to-earth welcome for Matt - she could sense he was close to being overwhelmed, and her father wasn't home yet.

'So, do you two ever work together?' she asked.

'We've only had the one trip together so far,' Elizabeth replied.

'It was Agadir,' Matt added.

'Lovely place, Morocco, some of my colleagues take their families over there for yoga retreats and rave about it. Well, honestly, anywhere with the sun and the beach suits me, I absolutely loathe the winter, don't you agree?'

She's nervous, Elizabeth thought.

'When I took the position in this hospital, I had to have a long hard think about living in London,' she added.

'Aren't you from London originally?' Matt asked.

'We are, but it's not the best place to work and you know... weather, and all that. But after all, home *is* home,' she concluded.

'You have a beautiful home,' Matt said.

'Thank you, we do try! Do you like my little collection of paintings?' Yvonne asked.

'They're interesting. I'm more into photography, though.'

'Who are your favourite photographers?' she asked.

'I always liked Henri Cartier-Bresson,' he said.

Yvonne jumped up in her seat.

'He was fantastic, what a pioneer!'

Elizabeth squirmed. *She's trying too hard.*

'Do you even know who he is?' she asked her mother.

'Of course I do, dear, we're not Philistines here!' she laughed.

'Do you play?' Matt asked, pointing at the piano.

'If you insist!' Yvonne said and sprang over to the keyboard.

She began to play a tune from memory, and Matt immediately recognised it as Philip Glass.

'The Candyman soundtrack,' he said putting down his Coke.

'Right!' she said in astonishment. Elizabeth you didn't tell me Matt was so knowledgeable!' she scoffed. 'See if you know this one.'

She started to play a very slow, romantic ballad with lots of ornamentation and closed her eyes.

'I don't recognise it, is it classical?' he asked.

'Not quite! It's something I've been working on for quite some time, but I never seem to get past this bit...' she started lingering on a minor chord.

'Oh stop showing off!' Elizabeth scolded her.

'I am not!' she said before pausing. 'I am quite proud of it so far,' she said.

'Tsk, where's dad?' she asked.

'It's quite beautiful,' Matt said, dropping the T in 'quite'. 'Elizabeth didn't mention you were into music.'

'Well, I have to say I'm curious about what she *has* been telling you!' Yvonne said, enjoying the playful atmosphere. 'We were all very astonished that Elizabeth didn't want to build on her history degree, but I *do* see the appeal of flying... Nevertheless, I know how hard you all work. I think hard work came as quite a shock to the system for my daughter, if you know what I mean.'

Matt put his arm around Elizabeth who smiled for the first time since they had arrived. Yvonne started leafing in a haphazard way through some of the sheet music that was next to the piano. From the kitchen the aroma of roast chicken and onions was filling the room slowly.

'That smells so good,' Yvonne said. 'I can't wait.'

Matt stood up again to take a look at the view from the window. When his back was turned, Yvonne slow-motion nodded her approval to Elizabeth who rolled her eyes and hoped Matt couldn't see in the reflection. Yvonne walked over to the sofa and used her index finger to push up the skin on Elizabeth's forehead.

'Oh mother, please,' she said instantly regretting it - she knew Yvonne could not help herself.

'It's still early, but soon...' she said.

'Soon what? You want me under the knife?' she asked.

'Nothing that drastic, but there are options!' Yvonne laughed. 'Let's not lie to ourselves about the course of nature... Are you eating properly? You need vitamins, green vegetables every day. And you can't drink enough water.'

'I know, I know! Stop it.'

Matt smiled and turned again to look at the beginning of the sunset.

'London *is* beautiful at this time of day,' Yvonne said.

Matt nodded. He had expected an expensive flat, but nothing like this. It was virtually palatial. He felt nervous that he might touch the wrong thing - almost everything in the apartment seemed to be an antique - and he was trying to avoid showing his unease. He was far from his comfort zone.

'Are you using the cream?' Yvonne asked.

'Yes!' Elizabeth whispered, exasperated.

'Just asking, precious. You mother loves you!'

'Have you been drinking?' Elizabeth asked.

Yvonne cackled and disappeared into the kitchen.

'I'm sorry about her, it's just her sense of humour,' Elizabeth said joining Matt at the window.

He gave her a peck on the cheek and she smiled to herself.

Yvonne came back holding a very large art book.

'Here we are. Cartier-Bresson, so vital, so influential!' she exclaimed holding out the book.

'This is my favourite,' Matt said holding it open on a page with a photo of a man holding his daughter in his arms. 'It's very simple, but it shows how, like, a picture can tell a story in a way words can't manage to.'

Yvonne and Elizabeth stood in silence looking at the picture. The shock in the man's eyes - or was it anger? - seemed too intense to keep looking at for too long.

'My pictures don't come close,' he mumbled.

The moment was interrupted by the front door opening.

'That's dad,' said Elizabeth.

'Daughter. Wife,' he said. 'Ah, are you the famous Matt? Nice to finally meet you!'

They shook hands. Michael's grasp was firm and he was enthusiastic to be meeting Elizabeth's boyfriend. He gave Elizabeth a big hug.

'Now that the introductions are out of the way, shall we

go to the dining room?' he said.

The room was enormous. The dining table was made of glass, ran the length of one side of the room and it had been laid, elegantly, in advance.

'Wow,' said Matt. 'You have a beautiful flat.'

'He's so *charming*,' said Yvonne aloud.

'Beautiful price, too. Don't ask. Property in London is insanity, pure insanity. I always said we should have taken something further out from the centre, or even commute from Europe, but Yvonne wouldn't listen,' he said.

'It's worth it if only for the convenience,' she chimed in.

'What did you think of Hounslow, dad?' Elizabeth asked.

'I think you're paying too much for a shared house, but the neighbourhood's peaceful enough. I just worry about you spending so much time near airports, the air pollution is shocking.'

'And the noise!' said Yvonne.

'You get used to it,' replied Matt.

'You do get used to it,' Elizabeth said backing him up.

'Wouldn't you love to be in your twenties again, Michael?' Yvonne asked. 'We were far too sensible at that age. If I had my time again, I'd have made the most of it!'

Michael pretended to shudder.

'Older and wiser,' he said.

Carmen came in with a huge platter of chicken. This was

followed by bowls of vegetables, warmed plates, condiments and a tray with a salad. After a few minutes she returned with bread and more sauces.

'Carmen, you're a genius, a goddess!' Yvonne enthused. 'Enjoy your meal, everyone.'

'Amen,' said Michael.

'Will Carmen join us?' Matt asked.

Elizabeth looked down at her top.

'Carmen's busy tonight, she'll be back in the morning,' Michael said trying to diffuse any embarrassment.

'Ah,' said Matt regretting his question.

'Sometimes we all eat together, Carmen's always been like part of the family,' Elizabeth said. 'James is staying over at his friend's house tonight, that's my baby brother, but he can be a bit of a handful.'

'Carmen is absolutely wonderful with James, she helps him with his homework. She's even taught him to do some cooking!' Yvonne said.

'Matt, are your family Londoners?' Michael asked.

'Yep, from near Hounslow actually, but I don't live with them. I moved out with my brother a few years ago,' he said.

'Do you come to central London much?' he asked.

'Oh, all the time. This is where it all happens.'

'We're thinking of going to see a play next week, you're both welcome to come,' he said.

'I'll have to see if I can get out of this medical conference that might overrun: it's some new gel, well, I won't go into it whilst we're eating, but anyway I'm ninety percent sure I can make it. Kim Cattrall from *Sex and the City* is in it,' Yvonne said. 'We all know your father has a soft spot for Samantha Jones!'

'It's true, it's true. I must have a thing for classy ladies,' Michael chuckled.

Matt and Elizabeth laughed.

Carmen came back with the champagne on ice and uncorked it unceremoniously. She served Yvonne first, and after taking a sip she was clearly on cloud nine.

'Oh my goodness, sublime, sublime. Matt please, you have to try this,' she said.

Matt held up his glass and Carmen poured.

'It's wasted on me, but...' he started.

He was nodding. The chicken, and the potatoes, and now the champagne were amazing. It was undeniably the best meal he had had for a long time, and in spite of the nerves, he was having a good time with his hosts. Yvonne and Michael were so friendly and welcoming that he felt as though he could never live up to their hospitality.

Michael slowly looked Matt over. He was a tall lad, and very polite. Compared with Elizabeth's ex-boyfriend Peter, the only other boyfriend he had met in person, he was confident. Peter had been a timid sort of chap, and this one had a bit more oomph about him. And he was obviously crazy about Elizabeth. Michael would not worry *too* much about this one.

Carmen returned one last time to turn on some soft background music on the stereo - it was choral music.

'It sounds like *heaven* in here!' Yvonne said.

'Good choice. Nice job, Carmen,' Michael said.

'Thank you,' she replied, returning to the kitchen.

'I hope you like the food,' Michael said addressing Matt.

'It's so good, thank you. So, Elizabeth said you work in the city.'

'For my sins, yes. I work for Morgan Stanley. Investments,' he said.

Matt had no idea how to reply, so he nodded.

'Deadly dull, but it pays the bills,' Michael said.

'I don't know how anyone can *bear* it,' Yvonne groaned.

'It can be fun. In a way.'

She was not convinced.

'Like I said, it pays the bills,' Michael argued.

'Matt, what do you think?' Yvonne asked.

'Mum stop it,' Elizabeth said.

Yvonne shot her a skeptical look and there was a silent pause.

'I wasn't trying to put Matt on the spot, I just think, well I *know* I couldn't work in an office. But so many people do,' Yvonne explained.

'Do you enjoy your job, Yvonne? It must be disturbing sometimes?' Matt asked.

'Oh I love it, I don't have a problem with gore at all! The thing is we just don't think about it. After the first few burns victims it came to be business as usual. I love surgery!'

'Cool,' Matt said. 'Did you always want to work in that area?' he asked.

'Pretty much, yes, I did. I always found surgery fascinating so that was the route I ended up taking,' she added.

The tension disappeared.

Matt looked over at Elizabeth and she took the opportunity to make a facial expression that said *I'm really sorry for this*. He winked at her.

'Do you have plans for the rest of the weekend?' Yvonne asked Matt and Elizabeth.

'We were going to chill out in Hounslow,' she said.

'How's that housemate of yours, the German one?'

'Sandra?'

Matt laughed.

'Have you met her?' he asked.

'Unforgettable. What's she up to?' Yvonne asked.

'We hardly ever see her these days, but when she's at home, you know about it!' Elizabeth said.

'She has a thing about being noticed, doesn't she?' Michael said.

'She was offloaded from a flight just before mum and dad met her for wearing glitter. The supervisor told her body glitter was not uniform standard.'

Matt scoffed.

'Don't judge a book by it's cover,' Michael said.

'Hear hear,' Yvonne said.

Matt finished his last piece of chicken. He had been gauging his intake because he wanted to avoid looking greedy; at the same time he wanted to show he was enjoying what was obviously an impressive meal. Yvonne topped up his glass.

'I'll show you some of my handiwork later, if you want. That is to say, if you're not too squeamish.'

'Oh Yvonne, he doesn't want to see third degree burns, it's not done,' Michael moaned.

'Matt is into photography, actually, and my patients were happy for me to record my work,' she retorted.

'Mum, it's a bit grim, come on,' Elizabeth said.

'I wouldn't mind...' Matt said.

'He's just being polite,' Elizabeth said.

'Cigarettes and coffee?' Yvonne asked, pulling out her gold-plated electronic cigarette.

'Yes, yes, cigar time,' said Michael, opening a tin box and pulling a blue glass saucer from the centre of the table.

Elizabeth went to the kitchen to turn on the coffee maker and collect some cups and sugar. She felt odd leaving Matt with her parents, but she was sure she had done the right thing by bringing him. He seemed at ease – as at ease as he could be expected to be under the circumstances - and he seemed validated in a way. As annoying as it was to admit to, she still valued her parents' approval. They had taken to Matt, and she was happy.

26

'The first thing you have to know about Sandra is that she is extremely German. The second thing is that she's not happy about the first thing,' Elizabeth whispered when she was out of earshot.

Paul smiled to show he had immediately understood. They were sitting in his room. He was on the bed and Elizabeth was perched on the small Union Jack beanbag. The garden door to the hallway next to the kitchen was open because it was already hot even though it was not yet the middle of the day.

Sandra strutted in as if on cue, wearing sequinned black leggings, her hair caked in cream bleach and a pink towel around her shoulders. The scent of the peroxide was overpowering.

'Hey, darlings!' she said peeking around the corner.

'Hi,' said Paul. 'New hair colour?'

'That's right! I'm going back to blonde. Brunette was so...' and she scrunched up her face.

'You're always changing your hair,' Elizabeth said with affection rather than criticism.

'Yes, I need to stay in style. Hashtag superstar!' she screamed.

Paul crept into kitchen to take the apple cake from the oven and placed it to one side on a cooling rack.

'Smells unbelievable!' Sandra boomed.

'Thank you, it's an old family recipe,' Paul replied. 'It needs sitting time,' he added.

Angela was upstairs. She was still in bed recovering from a twelve hour Larnaca duty, but Sandra seemed oblivious.

Paul turned on the tap to wash his hands, and the water spluttered. Then, there was no more water, just silence. He left his hands hanging there in the air.

'Is something with this tap?' Sandra asked.

'They were fine when I used them ten minutes ago,' said Paul, turning the taps on and off.

'Oh no,' Elizabeth said, stepping into the doorway. 'This again.'

'What happens?' Sandra asked in a frantic tone. The alarm on her watch started to beep.

'This happened before: they turned off the water for an hour to do repairs in the street.'

'But my head is covered in bleach! What can I DO?!' Sandra screamed at the top of her voice.

Upstairs, Angela's footsteps pounded across the landing floor as she marched to the top of the staircase.

'I'm trying to SLEEP!' she screamed.

The skin on Sandra's forehead was already beginning to redden, and she was breathing in and out loudly with the pain.

Angela stormed down to the corridor in a white dressing gown she had taken from a hotel.

'What the hell is going on? I need to sleep,' she said.

'I have to wash out... the bleach product from my hair... but the water is out,' Sandra explained.

Angela put her hand on Sandra's shoulder and marched her out to the garden.

'Stand there,' she ordered, picking up the bucket of rainwater that stood in the corner of the patio.

Sandra looked at the bucket in terror and started to cry.

'Kneel on the floor, we can rinse it out with this,' she said.

Elizabeth and Paul watched from the window and tried not to laugh.

'Aren't there cigarette ends in there?' Paul asked.

'Please, don't. I can't let her see me laugh,' she replied.

Streams of blue-white liquid poured from Sandra's scalp toward the lawn and she frantically scrubbed the bleach from her hair.

'Problem solved,' Angela stated as Sandra took deep breaths of relief.

Elizabeth took a tea towel from the kitchen to the garden and dried off Sandra's hair. She looked as if she was in shock, but stood up so she could see her reflection in the window. Paul waved. The colour was a very light blond, and she immediately forgot the trauma and started preening. A smile rushed across her face as she exclaimed, 'the perfect result'.

'It looks nice,' Paul mouthed through the glass with his thumbs up.

'You're welcome,' said Angela. 'I'm going back to bed.'

'Time for styling,' Sandra said, and headed to the kitchen to get her combs, hair products and her phone to take selfies.

'Of course when the water comes back I will do the deep conditioning, but the colour is a total perfection.'

Paul went outside to introduce himself.

'We have not met properly, I'm Paul,' he said, and held out his hand.

Sandra put her arms around him and gave him a big hug.

'So nice to meet you, I've been rushing around since I got back from Berlin, there is so much to organise,' she gushed in a whisper, as if suddenly remembering Angela was trying to sleep. 'You are from Poland?'

'Yes, I'm from Warsaw.'

'I love trips to Poland, I always get my extensions done there,' she replied beaming.

Elizabeth had never actually flown with Sandra despite having trained with her. Before her leave, the gossip was that she had been offloaded from a duty because the Captain said her fake eyelashes were ridiculous - they were far too long and unprofessional. She had argued back and refused to take them out, and this meant trouble because of such a flagrant breach of protocol. Whether the version of events crew told each other was accurate or not, Sandra had decided to use all her leave to take a break from the - mostly self-inflicted - 'stress of flying'.

'What is this?' Sandra asked Elizabeth through the window, pointing at the paddling pool box.

'Oh it's a pool, do you want to try it out?'

'Coool, yes.'

Paul was given the duty of using the flimsy plastic air-pump to inflate the thing, and by the time it was full of air, the water supply had been turned back on. Elizabeth took the hose and switched on the garden faucet.

'It's a lot bigger than I expected,' Elizabeth said.

'It's fantastic,' said Paul.

Angela re-emerged at the back door and laughed.

'That thing is ridiculous, the water bill is going to be double,' she said, before going into the kitchen and bringing out a CD player and box of cigarettes.

'Let me get changed,' said Paul.

'Me too,' said Sandra.

Angela sat on a plastic chair and lit up a cigarette. She had cheered up and looked relaxed.

'What's your next duty?' Elizabeth asked.

'Just Edinburgh there-and-back tomorrow, nothing major, thank God. I thought last night would never end. We had about twelve PRMs - it's the Paralympics or something. When are you back at work?'

'Not till...'

She was interrupted by the sudden arrival of Sandra wearing nothing but a neon yellow thong, and Angela burst out laughing.

'Sandra, don't you think...' she started.

'I need vitamin D. I'm sure Paul is no pervert!' she said with indignation. 'Why are you laughing, Angela?' she asked with genuine curiosity.

'I'm sorry, I just didn't expect you to... Never mind.'

'I'm very happy with them, it took a lot of money for this,' she stated pointing at her gigantic breasts.

Paul strutted into the garden in his swimming trunks and tried to hide his obvious embarrassment by looking away from Sandra. She giggled and skipped into the pool.

'It's fucking freezing cold!' she screamed.

'What did you expect?' asked Angela.

Elizabeth stuck her hand into the water.

'Maybe I'll wait a bit for the sun to warm it up before I get in,' she said.

'Come on, Elizabeth, be brave!' Paul said, slowly lowering himself in. She went inside to get into her swimming costume.

Sandra threw her head back on the side and allowed her hair to sit over the edge of the pool, basking in the sun.

'Be careful you don't burst the pool with your fake nails,' Angela said exhaling smoke.

'Don't worry, bitch,' Sandra snapped, sarcastically admiring her acrylic nails. 'Oh, by the way, are you sure it is safe for you to be around us while we're in a pool?' she quipped.

'Very funny,' Angela sighed.

When Elizabeth was changed, she checked her phone. There was a message from Matt inviting her to dinner in town with some of his old friends later that evening. She agreed, and told him he could pick her up at six.

She lowered herself into the cold water in the pool as carefully as possible.

'I'm going to town tonight for dinner with some of Matt's friends,' she said.

'Uh-oh,' said Angela, 'sounds like a test.'

'Oh no, it's not like that,' Elizabeth replied.

Angela scrunched up her face and put on a concerned expression.

'I'm sure they will like you,' Sandra said.

'What do you know about them?' Angela asked Elizabeth.

'Nothing, really. I suppose they're his friends from school. Or people he knows from doing up motorbikes?' she suggested.

Angela flicked some ash onto the patio.

'I didn't mean to worry you, but after him meeting your parents, this is another logical step,' she said.

'Yeah, but I guess I'm happy to be taking steps with him.'

'Ah, it's so romantic!' said Sandra. 'So, do you have a girlfriend?' she asked Paul as she stroked her hair.

Elizabeth shared a glance with Angela.

'Yes, we are engaged. I don't know when we will actually get married, though, we are still so young.'

'I agree, there is no point in rushing to fix your whole life, you have to just... go with the flow!' she said kicking her legs in the water. 'Can you take a photo of me?' she asked Angela.

'Why not,' she said.

27

The sun was beginning to set. Elizabeth stood by her bedroom window trying to ignore the sounds of the planes coming in to land in a queue. She looked out at the tree tops, the alley at the end of the garden, the tall houses that lined the main road.

It was half past six and Matt was late. She thought about the first time he had stayed over. In the time she had known him, he had never been late and she started to feel slightly anxious. The plan was to meet up at the house and head into town for dinner with his friends.

The doorbell finally rang and she headed down the stairs. Matt was standing there with another, slightly shorter, slightly younger version of himself.

'Hi, sorry we're late, this is my brother Anthony,' he said and gave her a peck on the lips.

'Hi, Anthony, nice to meet you,' she said.

He made an awkward shrug.

The tube journey into central London was long and full of uncomfortable silences. Every time Elizabeth tried to make small talk with Anthony, he seemed very guarded, as if he did not want to share much information about himself or his life, at least not with her. All she knew was that he shared a flat with Matt near the centre of Hounslow, he was looking for a job, had been for some time, and came across as quite depressed - she never asked if he actually was. Elizabeth wondered why Matt had brought him with them, but decided not to raise the topic in case she seemed insensitive. Worse was yet to come.

When they got to Piccadilly Circus, a plump, laddish man called Toby was waiting for them.

'Hey, Matt. Long time, no see,' he said and fistbumped Matt's hand. 'You must be Elizabeth,' he said, completely ignoring Anthony.

'Toby's a first officer at the airline, I don't know if you've flown together before?' Matt said.

'No, I don't think we have, nice to meet you. Where are we going for dinner?' she asked.

'It's a place just over the road, everyone's already there waiting for us.'

'Sorry, we've just been running a bit late,' Matt explained.

They walked over to Cruz's. It was a restaurant with a large bar, and lots of people were up dancing to the loud salsa music. Elizabeth was introduced to the rest of the numerous other people already drinking at the table. Apart from Toby, they were all cabin crew, but all new faces. Elizabeth ordered a white wine and some fries.

A woman called Kathy was holding court.

'We were coming in to land, and she still hadn't put a seatbelt on the kid... So, to cut a long story short, we had to do a go-around. I nearly fell over in the aisle when we shot back up. So when we finally landed, the captain was furious with this woman. They were talking about putting her on the no-fly list because she wouldn't back down or apologise'.

'Wow,' said Elizabeth, trying to get into the spirit. She could not mask a dejected feeling. She started to think she would have much preferred a quiet night with Matt, just the two of them. It was really tiresome to have to spend time outside of work inevitably talking about nothing *but* work; despite being in his company, she felt as though she missed Matt.

She felt something brush her hand beneath the table. She turned and saw Matt smiling across at her. He stroked her palm and she gripped his fingers slightly. He had sensed something was up.

Toby asked Anthony if he would be interested in working in aviation. He looked blank and then shrugged. There were a few titters from the rest of the table.

'Is your brother okay?' Elizabeth whispered to Matt.

'Yeah, he's always like this, don't worry. He gets a bit down sometimes.'

'Is there anything we can do?'

'No, he just gets like this. He's always been like that,' Matt explained.

Elizabeth sipped on her white wine, and tried to look like she was happy to be there since Matt was having a good time, but she was already beyond sick of hearing about flying - the same stories about difficult passengers retold again and again, and the complaints about the company and the rumours. The most annoying thing of all was when pilots and crew spoke as if they were expert economists discussing the business ins and outs of the airline. Did they really have any idea? She could not stop her frustrations from mounting up inside her.

Food started to arrive a little later, and Elizabeth made up her mind that she would leave after the main course with or without Matt, and risk being labelled anti-social, it was just too overwhelming. She went to the ladies room and texted him: 'Let's leave after the food? Stay over?'

By the time she got back to the table he had not replied but leaned over to her and whispered: 'Sure thing'.

* * *

It was the usual scenario: Matt staying over in Elizabeth's room. After dropping Anthony off near their flat, he couldn't keep his hands off her and she enjoyed the attention. Back in her room it occurred to her that although they had now slept together many times, neither of them ever ran out of ways to make it exciting. He hoisted her up into his arms and she allowed her legs to fold around behind him.

He held her back and pulled her in towards him, and as he firmly kissed her lips she moaned deeply. She slid her hand onto his lower back and playfully scratched at the top of his buttocks. His kisses sped up which she assumed meant he approved.

He pulled her underwear to one side very suddenly making her gasp. She hugged him tightly as he began.

'You like that!,' he teased.

'I like it. Go ahead,' she gasped and his speed and intensity increased.

Her thoughts swirled and wandered away as if she were in an ecstatic trance only returning quite some time later.

Elizabeth shook violently, breathless and sweating. Matt held her as he finished and she rolled over onto him on the mattress and lay there recovering in his arms.

'That was...' she started.

'That was fantastic,' Matt said in gleeful triumph.

28

The following day, as the sun had begun to set, Elizabeth got off the tube carriage when the doors opened at the terminal and took the lift up to the crew area which took up the first floor.

'Thanks dear, we'll call you when we need you,' the man at the front desk said handing her the miniature mobile phone.

Elizabeth walked over to the waiting room and sat alone on a sofa. The room was silent and a few people were trying to sleep, one woman looked up from her *Take A Break* and smiled at her although she didn't recognise her. In a company with over forty thousand staff most of the other crew were still strangers and likely to remain so.

She felt a tapping on her shoulders and spun round: it was Sandra holding out an identical phone.

'How long?' Elizabeth asked. 'I've only been here five minutes.'

'Only just arrived,' Sandra replied rolling her eyes. 'It's the not knowing... It's pain.'

'I was going to just watch TV until I get called... well, *if*...' Elizabeth said.

'We could have dinner in a while if we're both still here... Do you want to come to Dior with me?' Sandra asked.

'Sure,' Elizabeth shrugged.

They ambled over through staff security and into the Duty Free area airside. As soon as they started browsing the shop, Elizabeth's phone buzzed continuously and loudly.

'Hello?'

'Hi Elizabeth, briefing room 4 immediately please, you're on the Rome.'

'I'll be right there,' she said and hung up.

'Oh that is so not fair!' Sandra cried.

'Rome,' Elizabeth said. 'I haven't been there since I was a baby.'

'Life is so *un*fair!' Sandra went on, feigning a tantrum, but soon got back to examining the eyeshadows.

The briefing was ultra fast and the flight uneventful. The trip was an overnight with a late pick-up for the journey back so it meant that although she didn't exactly feel in the mood, she had a morning free to look around. The hotel was just a functional, beige 1970s Hilton; a grey pebble in a sublime garden. She set the alarm on her phone for nine, removed her makeup slowly and settled into bed just checking the phone once for a message from Matt, but he had not sent anything.

The next morning she opened the curtains and bright, warm sunlight flooded in. The hotel was very close to the city centre and she tried to take her mind off home for a few hours. She decided to go into the Colosseum which had small, narrow stairs made of stone. An elderly American tourist bumped into her as she was going up.

'She's going the wrong way,' the crotchety old woman stage-whispered to her husband.

When she got to the top, the view was incredible. The centre was a huge circle surrounded by long benches that made up the auditorium. In the areas behind the open part there were displays explaining the history. Elizabeth felt a little guilty. Sandra had texted in the morning to complain, having been stood down without a trip.

I should be enjoying this more, learning more, she thought.

The Roman Empire had not been one of her specialist areas, but she considered herself, in a way, to be a historian, and this place was beautiful and full of history.

She thought back to the houseshare. She thought back to Matt. She felt incredibly alone.

Walking back to the hotel, passing the ruins and statues which seemed to be scattered everywhere, she couldn't shake the feeling and started to think about what to do.

On the flight back she was distracted and got several drinks wrong in business class. Luckily the passengers were all in good moods and laughed it off - it was becoming more apparent as the months went by that 'air rage' was mainly an economy thing.

She took the tube back to the house and headed straight to the garden to relax a little. As soon as the door moved, she heard giggles, and when it was fully open she saw Angela crouching on the floor with Matt arranged on top of her.

29

As Elizabeth stepped backwards her legs felt weak.

'What is this?' she whispered. 'What's going on?'

'Elizabeth. Nothing, nothing, I'm just...' Matt started, standing to attention.

'Matt's just showing me how to ri-i-ide a motorbike!' Angela explained.

'Ride a motorbike,' Elizabeth said.

'Yes. Nothing for you to worry about,' Angela added with confidence.

After a long pause, Matt started to explain.

'It sounds stupid, it is stupid really. I think we've had a bit too much to drink, and...' he began.

'You've been drinking?' Elizabeth asked.

'Matt and I decided to finish off the Beaujolais, you're welcome to join us, honey. And you should take that look off your face, anyone would think we were doing something indecent,' Angela said.

'If I have a 'look' on my face it's because I've just come home to find my boyfriend... straddling my housemate,' she stated.

'He wasn't straddling me. Well, not in that way, it's perfectly innocent,' she replied with an undertone of indignation.

'Elizabeth, there's nothing going on, let me explain if I

can,' Matt added with a bright red face.

Angela picked up her glass of wine and gulped down what was left of it. It was disturbing to Elizabeth that she seemed to be enjoying the drama.

'I wouldn't have expected you to overreact like this, but when I think about it,' Angela began, 'what with the pool... and now the way you act around me these days, it actually makes sense. *You* are a very jealous person.'

Matt squirmed. Elizabeth suddenly felt enraged at this open provocation and moved slowly and carefully towards Angela. She slapped her hard across the face. Angela let out a loud yelp.

'What are you DOING you stupid bitch?!' she screamed.

'Nothing you don't deserve! Fuck both of you,' Elizabeth snarled before turning and running out of the garden, up the stairs and slamming her bedroom door behind her. From up there she could hear Matt consoling Angela.

'You bastards!' she kept repeating to herself, and before she knew it, there were tears streaming down her cheeks onto her uniform jacket. She blinked and looked over at her unmade bed. Matt started knocking on the door. She opened it carefully.

'Elizabeth you really have to hear me out. Nothing was going on, you've really overreacted here.'

'Have I?' she sobbed. 'What the hell am I supposed to think? Why would you even...?! I can't imagine...'

She kept at a distance from him and collapsed onto the floor, her uniform skirt tearing as she did. When she looked up she could see Matt's youthful face had gone from red to a greenish white. He looked ill.

'Don't just stand there, get out!' she said.

'I'm not leaving,' he replied and walked over, let out a deep breath and sat down on the floor beside her.

'I know what you think you saw, but you have to believe me, nothing is going on. I'm not that kind of person,' he said.

'What kind of person are you? Why didn't you call me yesterday or even send a text? What's going on?' she asked.

'Nothing's going on, nothing at all. Every couple has their ups and downs but I'm not, and have never been interested in Angela, absolutely not in *that* way. We're just friends, and I'd like us all to be friends. It seems a bit late in the day for that, but... I only came over here to surprise you when you got back.'

'I know it sounds selfish, but I want you to myself. And if you want to see someone else...' she started.

'I don't want to see anyone else. Elizabeth, when we first met, when we first went out, I knew there was something special going on. Something was... in the air. I can't tell you what made me feel that way, but in the time I've known you it has never stopped being amazing.'

She looked into his eyes and mopped her face with her sleeve. Nobody had ever spoken to her in this way before, with such honest and sincere affection.

'I'm sorry I don't text all the time, but I do love you,' he concluded.

'You love me?' she asked.

Matt nodded and held out his hand. She took it.

'I... I love you too,' Elizabeth said, fresh tears streaming down her cheeks.

He leaned over and put his hand on her shoulder. They looked deep into each other's eyes. Matt's eyes had never seemed so deep brown before, and she started to think how ridiculous she must have looked to him.

'I must look a complete mess,' she said whilst pulling at the torn area of her skirt.

'You look beautiful, come here,' he said taking her in his arms, kissing her softly.

She could taste the wine on his lips, and as they started to caress each other her phone buzzed in her pocket. It was a text message from Angela: 'Don't bother trying to say sorry for this - you are finished bitch.'

She turned the screen to show Matt.

'She'll get over it,' he said. 'It's a simple misunderstanding.'

'Not this time. Not this time,' Elizabeth whispered as a look of consternation crossed her damp face.

The sound of stones hitting the window made Elizabeth turn and stand up to see what was going on.

'Did you get the message? Read it, it's in plain English. You are finished! Ha-ha! There's no going back, DONE!' Angela shrieked up at her window. 'The police are on their way. That's right, *you're going to jail now* you stuck-up slag!' she cried. 'Common assault!'

'Angela, stop it, please, you're acting like you're in a soap opera or something,' Matt said.

'Go on then, go to your slut! Did she tell you she's screwed half the pilots in the company? Whoops, did I say too much? She didn't let you know THAT particular little factoid, did she?' she yelled out devoid of any self-consciousness.

Some of the neighbouring garden doors had started to open and people were trying to watch the spectacle unfolding.

'Yeah, I might be drunk, but I'm not so DUMB that I don't know your kind: how should one put it?' she sniffed. 'How about 'holier-than-thou little slag', that's an accurate label, isn't it? You have the NERVE to lay a hand on ME-E-E! You're DONE!' she snapped, and Elizabeth could hear her newly-enraged housemate stamping up the stairs.

'DO-O-ONE!' she wailed at the closed bedroom door in her drunken rage. Matt jumped. She slammed her own bedroom door and loud rap music started to pound away.

'Could you please get her to stop screaming and turn that shit down!' Brenda, their neighbour yelled up at Elizabeth's window. 'I don't know what you kids are playing at but some of us have work to to do. Please!' she added.

'Sorry about this Brenda,' Elizabeth replied. 'Matt, you don't think she really called the police, do you? I didn't assault her, it was just... I just lost my temper,' she started. 'And I haven't done what she said, she's just drunk and...'

'I can't think with that music blaring. You *did* slap her pretty hard,' he said.

'Oh God, this is ridiculous,' she said.

As soon as she finished the sentence the doorbell started ringing and outside a concerned pair, a man and a woman in police uniforms, stood waiting to see what was going on.

Matt and Elizabeth sat opposite each other in the Treaty Centre café drinking coffees.

'I can't believe she called the police on me,' Elizabeth said.

'To be fair, you did hit her hard. I was quite shocked,' he replied.

It was not normal for Elizabeth to ever behave violently, but she had snapped, and just as before during the wet drills in recurrent training, Angela had pushed her buttons. The solution seemed obvious.

'I'll have to move out, we can't both live there, it's like a disaster waiting to happen. I should've been able to predict all this. The things she said, she meant them. Whatever I do she'll always see me as stuck-up, but you know it's not true. I'm not like that. I don't feel superior to anyone, it's all in her head.'

'And me having anything to do with her aside from just being friends was all in *your* head,' he replied.

'Well touché, well done. But seriously, I don't know how anyone can have known me this long and think I'm some kind of snob,' she said.

'I guess we often see what we want to see and don't question it,' Matt said.

'There's no excuse. And I'm not making excuses for myself, but I don't trust her and she doesn't trust me. There's just no going back. I've got to move out of there.'

'And where are you going to go?' he asked.

'No idea. It has to be close to the airport but everything in the house is messed up now. Conclusively messed up,' she added.

'That's putting it mildly. You should move in with me,' he suggested.

'It feels early to be talking about moving in together,' Elizabeth explained. 'That was a bit insensitive,' she added. 'What I mean is, I do love you. I love you, but I like us having our own space. You know I don't want to risk everything by rushing. Oh, I don't know what I want really. Why is life always so unpredictable and messy?' she asked.

'You can't complain. In all the chaos you find out what really counts,' he said grabbing her hand.

She smiled.

'I think it's finally time you came and visited me and my brother in our flat,' Matt said.

'You said it's poky and out-of-the-way. I thought you never wanted me to see it in case it damages your image.'

'It is poky and, yeah... not great, but you're going to have to see it sooner or later. No time like the present, and no pressure to move in.'

'I'd feel nervous meeting your brother on his own turf. I'm sure he wouldn't want me moving myself in,' she said. 'I don't think he even likes me.'

'How do you think I felt meeting your parents?' he asked.

'My parents are lovely people,' she said.

'Ouch!'

'Oh, come on, that's not what I meant. Anthony is... Anthony. He's his own person,' she explained.

The gargling of milk frothing in the espresso machine drowned out the music in the shopping centre and Matt covered his ears.

'Well he is a bit miserable, but it's understandable...'

'Oh?'

'I won't bore you with the details, but basically he has never really found what it is he's passionate about. Maybe he never will. He was never any good in school, and so when he left he just went through a few menial jobs, a bit like me, but well... He took our parents' divorce much worse than me. He's had a hard time.'

'Family,' Elizabeth concluded.

'Family,' Matt repeated, looking at Elizabeth seriously.

'I'm not really happy about having to move, but there's really no option. I feel stressed out just thinking about it, but staying would be madness,' she said.

'There's no pressure from me, I just want you to be happy,' he said.

'Where am I going to find a place as cheap as the houseshare? I don't see any point paying out half my salary for some flat I'll hardly ever be in. When I started out, I was debating just staying in hotels near the airport but it adds up.

And it's not exactly convenient,' she frowned.

Matt put his coffee to one side and leaned over the table to kiss her. They grinned at each other - with him there, she realised, maybe she could handle anything.

'Whatever I decide to do it needs to be quick, I can't stay in that house with her on the loose, this time it's not like before, I've never seen her so... unfiltered. She really hates me on a deep level.'

'You're paranoid, some people get affectionate when they're drunk, and some... just become aggressive. I'm not saying you can make up, or *should* make up, but well... The alcohol played a big part in what happened.'

'Mhm? Some people get affectionate?' she said.

'Oh come on, not this again. I wasn't doing anything you wouldn't approve of.'

'Well you didn't exactly explain what you were doing,' she said.

'Nothing. Zero.'

He muttered something about passenger restraint training which somehow got onto the topic of motorbikes and Elizabeth rolled her eyes.

'I don't want to sound like a jealous wreck, but it did sting,' she said. 'Women want what other women have.'

'It was just a misunderstanding. I want you to trust me, that's what I value,' he said.

'I do, too. And I do trust you, Matt. I would never cheat

on you,' she said.

'Glad to hear it! Don't you think it goes without saying?'

'No,' she sulked.

'Elizabeth, you're the only girl for me!' he said.

'I won't ever tire of hearing it. Make sure you remind me constantly!' she laughed, finally, trying to lighten up.

Matt drank down the rest of his coffee. Elizabeth looked around.

'I sometimes think I'd really like to just get out of this place,' she said.

'The Treaty Centre?' he asked.

'Hounslow... London... You come back from somewhere like Rome and you just think...'

'What is my boyfriend doing on top of my housemate?' he suggested.

'I'm not ready to laugh about it! I just mean, it's so grim sometimes, even in summertime. It brings you down, and I'm not being a snob, but it's like the default reaction would be misery. Do you know what I mean?' she asked.

'I know what you mean, there's no getting away from it. But it is kind of my home. There's no place like home,' he said.

'Thank you Dorothy, but home should be a happy place,' she nodded.

'Let's visit my flat. I think Anthony is out today actually,' he said picking up his phone.

'I'll visit, I can't say I'm not curious. Where is he, anywhere nice?' she asked.

'I think he's at the cinema. He tends to watch the same kind of superhero things all the time. The same film multiple times,' Matt said.

'Ah.'

'All I meant is, when he likes something, he really likes it,' he explained. 'He's not *slow*,' he added.

'I didn't mean to say... Oh, I'm just going to keep my mouth shut, I can't open it without pissing everyone off.'

Matt kissed her again.

'Let's go! I haven't tidied up but you can have a poke around and finally see one of my beautiful bikes.'

'Oh I can't wait!'

* * *

What Matt referred to as the flat turned out to be a small, suburban terraced house. The tiny living room had walls covered in mostly black and white photos.

'Did you take all of these yourself?' she asked.

'I did,' he said, and paused. 'It's so weird you being here,' he added.

'It's not like I expected, you undersold it,' she said.

'What did you expect?! Cockroaches and water dripping from the ceilings?'

'Of course not, it's just very modern. Inside at least,' she said.

'It's Anthony who did all the painting work to the interior,' he said. 'Let me show you upstairs.

They walked to the top and Matt opened a blind and then the window.

'Airing the place out a bit. That's Anthony's room, and this is my room,' he said.

Inside Matt's room she was pleased to see a photo he had taken of her in a silver frame on the dresser, and next to it a photo of the ducks from their date in Richmond.

'It is small, but it's nice what you've done with the space,' she said.

'Good things come in small packages,' he said.

She looked him up and down.

'You're very modest,' she giggled, and sat one the bed.

He leaned over her and they kissed. She slouched back and undid her top. Matt ran his hands over her chest and she purred.

'Here?' he asked.

'Here,' she replied.

As they kissed, stopping every now and then to remove another item of clothing, the door opened quietly and slowly.

'Anthony! What the hell!' Matt cried out in a high pitch.

He stood up and marched out into the corridor. Elizabeth could hear them arguing but could not make out what was being said. For the second time that day she felt deeply embarrassed and out of place.

31

Dear Judith,

My wife has been suffering from depression on and off for the last ten years. There doesn't seem to be anything I can do to help her. She was fired from her job as a secretary five years ago, and since then she has been out of work. When I suggest doing things to alleviate the mood, she just shrugs and prefers to do nothing. Even though she was fired, there wasn't any one thing that triggered her depression, it just came about. Now we are both suffering because of it. Any suggestions would be greatly appreciated.

Justin, Wimbledon.

Well, Elizabeth thought, without bothering to read through Judith's reply, *what can you do? If someone doesn't want to be helped...* Of course she had Anthony in mind when she read this problem. *It's not easy to solve and it's not easy to be the one who is depressed, either,* she summed up, putting the book into the last of the boxes and ordering an Uber on her phone.

After the the interruption at Matt's flat, she had decided to move into her own place slightly closer to the airport. True, it was on a roundabout near two motorways that were constantly busy, but the price was unexpectedly low, and the commute to the airport would just be a short bus ride. Conveniently there was a Marks and Spencer's opposite too.

Whenever she started to feel depressed, she would feel a sort of guilt for doing so. She had grown up in a well-off, stable, loving family, and she had succeeded academically. Now she had Matt, so what should she really have to be depressed about? But still, as soon as one problem was solved, another seemed to crop up to take its place.

For the first week in the new flat she had no idea where to put her rubbish bags, and there were a lot of things she was throwing out that the previous tenants had left behind. That junk ended up gathering in the box room which she wanted to eventually use as a sort of storage room for her clothes.

When she texted the estate agent to ask about it, he just told her to ask another resident in the building where the recycling bins were, but they never seemed to enter or leave. It was very quiet, and somewhat *too* quiet. There seemed to be no children at all, no signs of life aside from a door closing now and then, and no housemates to chat to when she had time off.

Sandra had said she would visit one day but she was unreliable, of course. Paul wanted to go out for a coffee with her but there was no solid day and time fixed, and she seemed to be out of the loop. There was still Matt, but he didn't seem keen to spend too much time in the new flat. He felt bad leaving Anthony to see her, which made sense to him but always angered her.

As for Angela, they were not on speaking terms, and, Elizabeth thought, never would be again.

Two weeks into living in the new flat and Elizabeth had a group of three consecutive days off. She decided to do go into central London to do some kickboxing. It had been long enough and she didn't want to fall into the habit of not going again. She also felt an unexpected but overwhelming urge to be away from her new flat, and away from Hounslow. She wanted escape.

* * *

From behind the desk Bob greeted Elizabeth and looked happy to see her after the weeks of absence.

Elizabeth came down the concrete stairs mentally ready to kick and punch.

'We miss you when you leave us,' Bob said.

Elizabeth paid and warmed up on a punchbag when Chip arrived.

'Hey,' he said.

'Oh hi, it's Chip isn't it?' she asked.

'Chip, yes. The air traffic controller,' he said. 'Want to partner up? For pair work I mean,' he said.

Elizabeth nodded.

After the class he offered her a lift back to Hounslow since he lived in Twickenham, not too far away, and she accepted.

'You seem a lot happier than last time,' he said as they reached her new flat on the roundabout.

'I think you should know I met someone, I just don't want you to get the wrong idea,' she said. 'We're very happy, but then

I have to come back home here,' she said gesturing at the driveway.

'We can't have everything,' Chip said.

He looked slightly sad.

'You're a nice guy,' Elizabeth said before getting out of the car. 'And a good sparring partner,' she added.

He smiled accepting the situation and waved at her before driving off.

32

Back at work, Elizabeth felt somehow shaken, but she was trying to put everything that had happened behind her. It was not easy to do at the airline when everything around her reminded her of Angela, her old houseshare and throwing herself into work seemed to in fact be the opposite of a fix-all solution.

'Are you ready to do the service?' Donald asked.

'Sorry, I was...' Elizabeth began.

'You were in a world of your own. What are you daydreaming about?' he asked.

'Nothing, just personal stuff,' Elizabeth replied.

It was pure torture to be flying with Donald West again, and especially annoying this early in the day. Donald had not changed a bit, and if anything seemed to have only got worse since the first time she had flown with him.

He had remembered her from the Manchester duty and on this occasion he seemed to be particularly paranoid about upsetting the passengers in some way. It occurred to Elizabeth that most of the passengers could not care less about who was serving them, as long as they got their complimentary toasted cheese and ham sandwich and a gin and tonic before landing in Oslo.

'Well let's try to keep the personal personal, and put the customer first, please,' Donald replied without a hint of good humour.

'Right,' said Elizabeth standing up from her crew seat

which folded away and swung open the door of the trolley where the plastic crates of sandwiches were stowed during take off.

'We mustn't dilly-dally, there's no time to waste on these short there-and-backs,' Donald shot before springing back to the front of the aircraft.

As soon as Elizabeth started the service from the curtain divider, she slipped back into her daydreaming. She pictured Angela's face bearing a devious expression that left no doubt about her motives; a false memory, but a vivid image nonetheless.

'I asked for no ice in the orange juice,' the woman in sunglasses snapped.

'Oh, I'm so sorry,' said Elizabeth taking back the drink from her tray table.

'I specifically said none,' the woman added with a smirk before looking at her husband as if to say 'Can you believe this?'

'Here you are,' Elizabeth said, holding out the correct drink for which she was not thanked.

As she progressed speedily down the aisle, she heard a man murmuring. He tapped her on the back and she knelt down to hear what he was saying.

'You should smile more,' he said.

She frowned and finished the service, with just enough time to put everything away.

She sat at the back with the door open as the passengers disembarked, thanking each one with the customary rehearsed, fake smile. After they had all left down the metal staircase and the cleaners were coming up, Donald returned to the back of the plane to dispense some more words of wisdom.

'I've been in this business a long time,' he started. 'If there's one thing I've learned it's that the customer is always right. You can't say the same about those bastards in the flightdeck, but as far as we're concerned, the customer comes first,' he finished before darting off.

Elizabeth had heard similar lectures and the same tired clichés many times before and she just felt bored. Donald no longer intimidated her, he was just an annoyance, a persistent pain, and it was an effort to fake the smiles and 1960s customer service that were expected. She wondered what Matt was doing in his hotel in Taipei. He was probably out with his cameras trying to capture as much as he could at a night market, perhaps.

'Here you are darling, do you want some of these?' Beverly, the third crew member on the duty asked.

She was holding out a little tray of pastries that she had managed to smuggle down from business class.

'No, thank you,' Elizabeth said.

'Well you have to eat something, this was an early start. Maybe that's why you look so sad. How do you think *I* feel up there in business working with *that* prissy bitch?'

'Do I look sad?' Elizabeth asked.

'You look like you could do with cheering up. None of us like these early there-and-backs, well except for the women in the 'Breakfast Club', but I can tell you hate it. Don't let it wear you down, keep your strength up. We'll keep up a united front against you-know-who.'

Elizabeth took a pain au chocolat and poured out two coffees. Over the PA system the Captain announced that the passengers were due in ten minutes.

'Only about two hours to go, thank God. Remember: don't let the bastards get you down,' she advised.

Elizabeth was unsure if she was referring to people like Donald or the passengers, but either way, the Oslo on the first day back was an ordeal.

* * *

The next day, Elizabeth was rostered a taxi to Birmingham. She would be driven to a hotel there and have to do Munich there-and-backs for two days before being taxied back to London. It was not something she was looking forward to, but at least it was a stay somewhere new and outstations tended to have nicer crew. The hotel was near a conference centre and when she entered the lobby she could see there was a huge swimming pool in the spa area behind a large, open restaurant and it looked new and shiny. Her mood started to lift.

'Oh no, it's you,' said a familiar voice.

'Matt!' Elizabeth squealed. 'What did...?'

'I took three days of leave and shared an earlier taxi with another crew so I could stay up here with you. If... that's okay,' he said.

'Of course it's okay! Come here,' she said and grabbed him for a big hug. They began to kiss and Matt eased off, wary of creating a scene.

The receptionist who had checked her in was watching everything and started to smile.

'You're in room 242, lucky for you it's a honeymoon suite,' he said.

'Fantastic,' said Elizabeth taking the keycard.

'Enjoy your stay,' the receptionist said. 'Both of you,' he added.

'Let's see this suite,' said Matt, helping her with her luggage as they walked to the lifts.

* * *

Matt did some lengths of the pool before swimming over to the attached jacuzzi where Elizabeth was relaxing alone in the bubbles.

'So do you want to go into town?' he asked.

'Not really,' she said. 'I could stay here all day, it's so relaxing.'

'Lady of leisure.'

'I just don't see any reason to go into the city, this hotel is so nice.'

The reception area, just visible from the pool, had

become busy because the hotel was hosting a recruitment event for a smaller local airline.

'I'm happy anywhere it's with you,' Matt said looking a bit embarrassed although he clearly meant what he was saying.

'Matt!' Elizabeth squealed splashing him with water.

'Stop!' he scolded.

Elizabeth watched the prospective cabin crew in the hotel lobby looking nervous and she could see in their eyes that they all wanted the job just as badly as she had done.

Back in the suite, she and Matt had a long talk. She explained her dislike of the new flat. It had been a mistake. Finally they agreed she would live with Matt temporarily to test the waters.

'If you can put up with Anthony. And me,' Matt said.

'I think I can manage,' she said.

She grabbed the back of his neck and gently pulled his head to hers. He inhaled the faint scent of chlorine that lingered on her hair and she gazed at him with her eyes open.

They made love.

'It's the start of autumn,' Matt said.

It had to be acknowledged that the cooler weather had begun. As he looked down at Elizabeth who was lying next to him in his garden he felt a touch of protectiveness towards her.

'It's beautiful out here. I'm not cold' she replied.

'You don't regret moving in here with me and Anthony, then?' he asked.

'Well,' she started, looking around at the building, the grass and the motorbike parts lying around them. 'Well, it could do with a bit of tidying up, I think it'd be worth it.'

'A woman's touch?' he asked.

'A bit of something or other, but it's a really good start,' she said. 'As for Anthony... he's no trouble really,' she concluded in a whisper.

He leaned down and kissed her on the forehead.

'I can put up with it all,' she said.

'For now,' he joked.

'For now. Realistically, how much time are we going to spend here anyway? My parents like having you over, and we can sync up our rosters,' she suggested.

'Rosters – God, I'm so sick of hearing words like that. Rosters, crewing, always the same stuff. I can't wait to get out,' he said.

'You will. You can do anything you want. When we were in Birmingham and there was the recruitment day for crew I was thinking if I'm even sure I want to keep flying... always being in a different part of the world all the time,' she said. 'Well those bits are okay, it's the two and four sector days that stick the knife in. Maybe I should get a bit more *serious* about life.'

Elizabeth pulled out a magazine from the small pile she had beside her.

'If you are thinking about marriage or something like that, just stop right there!'

She laughed and put the magazine to one side.

'So you don't really love me?' she joked.

'It's a bit early for... You know,' he started.

She sat up fully and laughed, put her arms around him and kissed him slowly. Matt returned the gesture and she melted into his arms.

'I was kidding, I'm so happy like this,' she said. 'And I wasn't hinting at anything where we are concerned. I wouldn't change a thing.'

A plane flew overhead.

'Doesn't it always spoil everything?' he asked, looking up.

'No. Every time I see one I think about how lucky I am,' she replied. 'It's how we met.'

'I'm the lucky one. Well, you just never know where anything is going to lead, do you?'

'Exactly,' she concluded. 'If it wasn't for you, I'd probably be miserable.'

She grasped her hands together in a lighthearted way.

'It's just a matter of time before I figure the rest of my life out!' she said.

'Elizabeth... Thank you. I really mean that. And I'm glad we did. Meet, that is,' he said, now wearing a very serious expression on his face.

'Shh,' she said, 'just keep thinking positive.'

'It's easy to do when I'm with you,' he replied.

She squeezed him in her arms and patted his head before he reciprocated, sharing a long, passionate embrace.

'Let me tell you what I believe,' she said coming up for air. 'The sky's the limit.'

I would like to say a huge **THANK YOU** *to my family and friends who have been an unending source of love and support, helping me in ways big and small with the creation of this book. Every one of you means the world to me, and your help has never gone unnoticed or unappreciated.*

I would particularly like to thank Simon Griffith for his early tips which convinced me to continue developing this novel, Craig Ewens, Kevin McNamara, and Stephen Tate.

I could not have done it without you. From the bottom of my heart, thank you!

- Jamie O'Neill, 2020.